Pippa
Goodhart

The
Twisted
Threads of
Polly
Freeman

For my very good friend Maggie
who lived the writing of this book
with me on many dog walks.

CATNIP BOOKS
Published by Catnip Publishing Ltd
320 City Road
London
EC1V 2NZ

This edition first published 2020

3 5 7 9 10 8 6 4 2

A CIP catalogue record for this book is available from the British Library.

ISBN 978-1-91061-122-7

www.catnippublishing.co.uk

The
Twisted
Threads of
Polly
Freeman

Pippa Goodhart

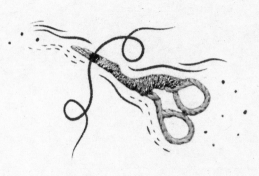

Chapter 1

London, 1838

'Oi, you!'

Polly clenched her fists. She didn't turn, and she kept on walking as she heard the big, rustling skirt of Mrs Proudfoot scurrying up behind her.

'Don't you walk away from me!' said Mrs Proudfoot. Polly forced her mouth to smile as she turned to face the woman.

'Oh! I didn't know you was talking to me, Mrs Proudfoot,' she said, eyes wide. 'I do hope that you and Mr Proudfoot are well?'

'Vermin, that's what you are!' said Mrs Proudfoot, grabbing Polly's arm and pinching it viciously. Polly glanced to where people were turning to watch the well-dressed woman shouting at the barefoot girl. Realising that she had an audience, Mrs Proudfoot let go of Polly.

'This girl and her aunt live in my basement, and they owe me rent,' she said.

That was true. In the long cold winter, Polly and her great-aunt hadn't been able to earn enough to keep up with the rent as well as with buying enough food and coal to keep themselves alive. They'd paid off some of what they owed as the year warmed and made earning a living easier, but they did still owe several shillings.

'You'll get the rest of it,' said Polly fiercely. Mrs Proudfoot did a fake laugh.

'I ask you,' she said. 'Would you believe this girl if you were me?' The man and two women who had stopped to watch looked down at scruffy Polly with her wild thick black hair and dark skin, and their sneery laughs made clear that they wouldn't. 'And as for the scraggy old spinster,' went on Mrs Proudfoot. 'She . . .'

'At least she doesn't shout rude things at her husband like what you do,' said Polly, glaring.

'Whatever do you mean?' said Mrs Proudfoot.

'D'you want to know what she said to him last night?' said Polly. She could see that they did. 'We hear it all through the floorboards when they have one of their spats. Mrs Proudfoot said to Mr Proudfoot that he hadn't as much brains as what a sausage had. And she said . . .' Polly put on Mrs Proudfoot's voice. '"Besides that, Alf, a sausage is better-looking than you are!"' The laughter turned on Mrs Proudfoot now. Her face reddened, and Polly suddenly knew with sick certainty that she had made a bad mistake. Mrs Proudfoot pointed at Polly.

'Pay what's owed by the end of tomorrow or I'm evicting the pair of you.' She tilted her nose upwards. 'The workhouse is where your kind rightly belong.'

The idea of being shut in a workhouse was the one thing that truly frightened Polly's great-aunt Jem, so it frightened Polly too. *We've got to get that rent money*, she thought as she ran home. *We've got to get it fast.*

The door at the bottom of the steps leading down from the road was already open. Inside their basement room, Aunt was sitting tall on a stool beside the small window of wobbly glass. Light coming through it fell on the sewing work on her lap. Polly pulled the door shut.

'What's ruffled your feathers?' asked Great-Aunt Jem, blue eyes looking sharply at Polly. 'Leave that door open to let the light in.'

Polly just pointed to the ceiling. 'She says we've to pay what's owed by tomorrow.'

'Oh, she's always saying that,' chuckled Aunt, cutting a length of pale thread from a small reel. 'We're paying her off, bit by bit, and she knows it. Blimey, we're sleeping on the floor because we sold our bed to get money for her. And we're working all the hours. Did you get anything?'

Polly bent down and reached under the skirt of her brown dress to take out the scabby and wilted outer cabbage leaves she'd picked up from under a market stall. She put the leaves into a pan.

Aunt made a face. 'That it?' Then she looked at Polly again. 'Has her upstairs said something particular to upset you this time?'

'No,' said Polly, turning her back and tipping water from the jug into the pan, and then over a basin to wash her hands before she started on her own needlework. 'But let's pay it all to her tomorrow if we can. Just to annoy her!' Polly paused. 'When does Mr Moser come next?'

Aunt and Polly's most regular work was sewing men's shirts for a man called Mr Moser, who brought them the cut-out fabric shapes to be stitched together. Aunt did the seams, joining the pieces. Polly was expert and fast at stitching neatly along buttonhole edges and cuffs and neck openings.

'Oh, you know him. He'll turn up when it suits him,' said Aunt. 'Might be tomorrow, might be next week. But what he'll pay us won't be enough to cover what's owed in any case.' She patted the upended wooden box beside her. 'Come on, Poll, get to work. If you finish that hankie this evening, we can go to the market tomorrow. You'll have three pretty hankies to sell then, and there's my rose too. That should make a bit. And the fella whose trousers these are is coming tonight and will pay me . . . or go without his trousers!' Aunt chuckled. 'See this?' she said, pointing to a faint line on the seat of the pair of cream-coloured twill trousers she had draped over her lap. 'I did that mend just last week when his dog first bit him on the bum. Now he's come back with another hole. Same dog, same bum, but a bigger tear. That dog had a good chew this time. I'm grateful to it for the work even if the fella isn't!'

Aunt was well known locally for her 'invisible mending' skills. Polly was embroidering a butterfly on the corner of a white cotton handkerchief. The handkerchief itself was made up of inch-wide strips of fine cotton cut from the bottom of bigger pieces of white fabric brought to be sewn into shirts. '*Nobody'll miss an inch*,' Aunt said. '*And we can use it*.' Polly stitched those strips together to make squares, then she and Aunt embroidered the squares' corners with flowers or other pretty things. '*Something special to draw the eye, so they'll never even notice how the handkerchief's been made*.' When they'd made enough of them, Polly and Aunt would stand just a step outside the market boundary, selling hankies from a basket. That way they didn't have to pay for a stall. It was usually men who bought the hankies as favours for the girl they fancied. They liked the flowers Aunt made from coloured fabrics too.

Polly sat on the box, a dead peacock butterfly placed on a scrap of white cotton on one knee, her white hankie square on the other. She threaded a needle with black thread ready to stitch-draw the butterfly's outline, and she peered closely at the dead butterfly. 'Those shapes on its wings look like eyes,' she said.

'That's its cleverness,' said Aunt. 'Those eye patterns trick birds that might want to eat it into thinking it's something bigger than it is, so they leave it alone.'

'Like when you pretend to be grand?' smiled Polly. She was thinking of the way Aunt would sweep haughtily into a shop where she wasn't known, choose a thing, then make a show of having lost her purse, all while talking with an upper-class voice. Sometimes the shopkeeper would be so eager to please what they thought was a rich customer, they'd let Aunt take the thing for free.

A slammed door above made Polly jump. Mrs Proudfoot was home. *Thump, thump!* A deliberate stamping of boots on the Proudfoots' floor, Polly's and Aunt's ceiling, made dust fall on to them and their work.

'Dear me, she *is* in a strop,' said Aunt, brushing a hand to sweep the bits of dirt off the cream trousers. *You don't know how true that is*, thought Polly. What if they really did get evicted? Polly looked around their dingy damp home. On a small table were five finished shirts, neatly folded, ready for Mr Moser to collect. There was one set of shirt pieces still to be worked, a tin of buttons, a big reel of white thread.

On the floor in one corner was a mattress of stitched-together sacking pieces stuffed with dried grass, bits of worn-torn cloth, and scrumpled paper scraps. 'It's a wonder we don't resort to putting dead rats in it too,' Aunt had sighed when winter froze the world around them. It was a lumpy bed, but cosy enough with both of them in it, warming each other. And they piled clothing on top of their old quilt. There was always a stack of clothes waiting to be worked on, along with a ragbag of precious good pieces of fabric taken from clothes when they got beyond repairing.

By the small fireplace was a shelf with pots and bowls, knives and spoons. There was another shelf up on the wall, away from mice. On it was a bag with a lump of bread in it, a jar of lard, and a few precious odds and ends; a fabric rose, a black velvet drawstring purse, Aunt's almost bald but once smart hairbrush.

'Were you ever truly grand?' asked Polly, wishing that

somewhere there might be rich relatives who could help them now.

'Not likely!' said Aunt, biting through a thread with her wonky teeth. 'Me dad and three of us lived in a place no bigger than this, and made mostly of mud and straw. It was owned by a mean horrible farmer we all worked for every moment of daylight. Then, when me dad died, that farmer wouldn't let us children stay, so it was the poorhouse for us unless we could find something better. I was the only one that did find something better. The others were dead within the year.' Aunt shook her head. 'I got to live in a big-grand place then, but I was a servant. Like a canary in a cage, I was fed and sheltered, but I had to please my lady, singing the songs she wanted, or I'd have been in the poorhouse myself.'

'What about your mother?' said Polly, turning her fabric as she worked around the butterfly-wing shape.

'Dead. I never knew her,' said Aunt.

'You're like me, then,' said Polly. *How would life be if I had a mother?* she wondered. 'Tell me about my ma,' she said. Aunt chuckled. They both knew what she would say.

'Your ma was a swan, Polly, as white as milk, soft as dandelion fluff, and strong as a poker.'

'And my dad?'

'Oh, he was a robin, that one. Red and brown and a fighter. And you, my Poll, are a sparrow. Small and brown and quick.'

'Sparrows are boring and dull,' said Polly. 'I'd rather be a colourful parrot like the one upstairs.'

'You don't want to live in cage like that poor bird,' said Aunt. 'Besides, just think, if you was red and green you'd catch the eye even more than you do now. Nobody much notices sparrows, and that's their cleverness. They're quicker than any big, bold bird when it comes to pecking up crumbs.'

'Shall I always be pecking up crumbs then?' said Polly.

'No,' said Aunt, jabbing her re-threaded needle back into the trousers' bottom. 'A girl as quick and clever with a needle as you are should be apprenticed to a dressmaker, Poll. Then you could make yourself a respectable, sure sort of a living.' Aunt sighed. 'But apprenticeships do cost a powerful lot of money.'

That thought jolted Polly back into worry about the

money they needed now. She looked up to the shelf where she could see a small, red velvet rose that Aunt had worked on for the last few days. It was beautifully done, with stitched leaf veins, and the petals and leaves all stiffened with starch so they were shaped like real ones.

'That's your best flower yet,' said Polly. 'You've got those middle little stick bits just like in a real rose.'

'Bristles from my brush,' said Aunt. 'Not many bristles left on it now. My lady gave me that brush many years ago as a reward for something.'

'What had you done to please her?' said Polly.

'Oh, I think I'd embroidered her favourite flowers, or some such. She did love her flowers, did Lady Burrell, and she taught me how to embroider. I think she chose me so young on purpose so's to teach me her ways with sewing. And with plants.'

'What ways with plants?' said Polly, selecting mauve from the box of small windings of different-coloured threads. That thread had been pulled from the hem of one of Aunt's mending-job skirts. Nobody noticed a single thread missing, but a thread like that could be turned into butterfly wings.

'Making medicines,' said Aunt. 'Mind you, not all of my lady's special plants made a person healthier. Some did quite the opposite.'

'Poisons?' said Polly.

'That's it. My lady told me we was making poisons for killing rats that were troubling the kitchens. Then her husband died, and some said that he'd died of poisoning. She had me burn all her plant books then. She got rid of me an' all. I suppose that was in case I told what I'd learned from her.'

'So had she . . .?'

'I never knew,' said Aunt. 'If she did kill him, she got away with it.'

'We could poison them Proudfoots,' said Polly.

'Don't you joke about such things,' said Aunt. 'If Lady Burrell had told the magistrates I'd killed her husband, they'd have believed her. They'd have hung me dead for certain sure, even though I never harmed the man.'

For a time they both worked on in silence. Then Aunt set aside the mended trousers, rose to her feet and eased her back. She looked down at Polly. 'I know you well enough to tell that there's something more that you've not told me, Poll.' So Polly told her about the threat of eviction.

'You see, we've *got* to get the money fast,' she said.

'Well, I do have an idea,' said Aunt. 'It would need us both to play our part, mind, and it could be risky.'

'What is it?' said Polly, heart a patter, hands still.

'You and I, Poll, must go fishing,' said Aunt, and there was a glint in her eyes as she explained exactly what she meant by that.

Neither of them slept much that night, restless through the hours of darkness. Polly reached out a hand, felt Aunt's bony hand take hold of it, and squeezed it reassuringly.

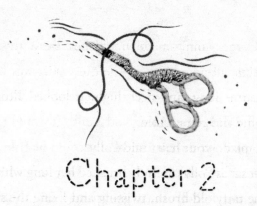

Chapter 2

At first light, Aunt took a big, stiff black dress from the pile of clothing in the corner. It had once belonged to a high-class lady, but the dress must have caught fire up the front because it was badly burnt. Aunt had cut out the burnt parts, replacing them with black fabric scraps, which she covered in a tumble of tiny, black-petalled flowers she had made.

Aunt shook out the dress now. It smelled faintly of the lavender that Aunt had snipped, leaning over somebody's front fence last summer. She'd folded the lavender into the dress to keep moths away. Now Polly helped to hold the dress open as Aunt bent down and dived into it. Then Aunt stood, letting the skirt tumble down over a home-made underskirt built from bits and pieces, all now hidden. The dress skirt was full, its bodice arms long, and neck high. It looked altogether handsome and respectable.

'Let me do your hair,' said Polly.

Aunt sat as Polly carefully brushed her long white hair with the tatty old brush, twisting and fixing the strands under a straw bonnet that had a small veil of fine black net that hid the top half of Aunt's face.

'Remember, keep your mouth shut tight,' said Polly. Aunt's teeth were wonky, one near the front missing altogether. But as long as she talked 'small' and didn't smile she now looked like a respectable widow.

'In mourning for the husband I never had nor ever even wanted,' laughed Aunt, mouth wide, then she put up a hand to cover it.

'Don't laugh!' reminded Polly. 'You're meant to be sad! And don't let her upstairs see you like this or she'll know we're up to something. I'll go up to the road first to check she's not about.'

There was no need for Polly to dress up. Her role in this was to be the invisible quick sparrow, so she was in the same plain brown dress as always, feet and head bare. Except that Aunt suddenly reached down the new red velvet rose and pinned it into the thick bounce of Polly's hair. 'It's only right you should be dressed a bit special too,' she said. 'You'll feel bolder, knowing it's there. If our fishing works well, you can keep that rose, Poll. If not, we can still sell it.'

When Polly went up the steps to the road there was no sign of life from the house above, so she beckoned Aunt to come out. Then they both hurried away from the place where they were well known, into a smarter street not far away. Carriages clip-clopped importantly past, and top-hatted gents and big-skirted ladies went about their business, mostly ignoring the girl offering matches and the coalman hefting heavy sacks from his cart.

'Now, Poll,' whispered Aunt, leaning close and pretending to put a coin into Polly's outstretched hand. 'Just remember that when I hook my finger, I'm . . .'

'. . . you're ready to start fishing,' said Polly. 'I know.'

'Right,' said Aunt. 'You hold back now, but keep a sharp watch.'

Polly moved to the side of the street, standing in the

shadow of the coal cart, and staying still.

Aunt looked magnificent as she walked away, very upright, carrying the black velvet drawstring purse from one wrist. Polly could see from the slight movement of her bonnet that Aunt was looking around for a likely gentleman 'fish' to catch. That velvet purse hung heavily because Polly had popped a couple of stones into it to give a weighty look that suggested it contained coins.

Suddenly Aunt changed course, walking towards a gentleman in a top hat who was on his own. The gentleman had a piece of paper in his hand and was looking at it in puzzlement. Polly was near enough to hear Aunt ask him in her most refined voice, 'Are you lost, sir? Might I be of assistance?' Polly, enjoying Aunt's voice, only just noticed that she had one hand behind her back, and that she was crooking its little finger. The hook!

Glancing quickly over her shoulder to check that nobody was watching her, Polly ran fast into the sunlit street, dashing past Aunt and snatching the dangling purse she was holding loosely from her fingers.

'Oh, goodness, no!' called Aunt in her refined voice.

'Hey!' shouted the man. Would he follow her? With the bag held tight in her fist, Polly hurried on, ears alert. But she could hear no footsteps running after her. Polly crouched behind some railings to look back. Aunt was 'swooning', crumpling down into the road, just as they'd planned.

'Oh, I've been robbed!' she wailed as she fell. And the man was doing exactly what Aunt had told Polly he was bound to do. He was reaching out to catch Aunt, so he couldn't follow Polly at the same time. Clever Aunt! Lifting and turning her skirt so that she could stuff the snatched purse into its secret pocket, Polly didn't see Aunt's next move. But she knew that one of her hands would be spidering into the man's coat to take what she could from him. *I've only ever picked the pocket of somebody who can afford to lose a little,* she'd told Polly often enough, and this man looked rich.

Polly was relaxing with the nice feeling that it had all gone just as they'd hoped, when shouting made her look back to the street. The top-hat man was still stuck holding Aunt, but that wasn't stopping him from trying to cause trouble for Polly.

'Stop, thief!' he shouted. 'I say, Constable, come here!'

Now Polly saw with a sharp spike of fear in her guts that a blue-uniformed constable was indeed running towards the man and her aunt.

'A wretched child has stolen this lady's bag!' said the top-hat man.

Clutching the railings, Polly hardly breathed as she watched and listened. She'd have made a run for it if Aunt wasn't stuck there with the man and the constable. Heart thumping high in her throat, Polly's legs were ready to flee if they had to. Aunt was getting to her feet, helped by the man, as the constable came up to them.

'Did you see the child who took the bag, ma'am?' asked the constable.

'Yes I did,' said Aunt, tugging down her veil as far as it would go, then wafting a gloved hand in front of her face as if she was still feeling faint. *Hiding those wonky teeth*, thought Polly. 'It were a boy,' said Aunt. 'A boy with hair the same lovely golden colour as your own, Constable.'

'It wasn't!' said the top-hat man. 'I distinctly saw a girl, with thick dark hair.' He was frowning at Aunt now. Both men were.

Aunt's posh voice saying, 'It were a boy,' rang in Polly's head. *They've guessed*, she thought. And Aunt clearly thought the same thing. Polly saw her snatch handfuls of the full black skirt, and begin to run. The gentleman, one hand to his hat brim, just watched her go. But the constable, momentarily taken by surprise, shouted and followed after Aunt . . . until Polly, running hard and with her head down, crashed into him, punching her head into his stomach, and winding him with a pleasing *oof!* sound.

Then Polly dashed off, zigzagging and nipping through small gaps, hoping to lead the constable away from Aunt, who couldn't run as fast as she could. *Get back home quick, Aunt*, Polly willed her. *Get out of that dress and hide it. Hide whatever it is you took from the man's pocket as well!*

Running hard, heads turning to watch her, Polly soon realised that nobody was actually following her. She looked back, and there was no constable there. That scared her. Where was Aunt? Had they got her? Please, please, please, no! Walking fast, skipping and running a bit, trying to look as everyday ordinary as a sparrow, Polly hurried homewards.

She heard the trouble before she saw it.

'Stop, madam!' shouted a man's voice. 'I must insist . . .'

Polly ran into their road to see the constable pointing to where Aunt, up on the front step of the main house where the Proudfoots lived, was looking as if she was about to open the door. The constable was bent over slightly, and panting out his words. Aunt must have run fast. Now she waved a hand imperiously at the constable below.

'Please leave me alone, young man. I am a respectable lady in mourning for my dear departed h—'

'Then why, madam, did you run?'

'Why?' Aunt pulled a finely embroidered handkerchief from her sleeve, and dabbed at her eyes. 'My husband is only recently dead, and I cannot abide upset of any kind,' she said. 'My nerves won't stand it! Now, please let me enter my home so that I can have the privacy

I desire.' Polly saw the constable hesitate. Oh, if only Aunt could actually go inside that house . . .

Suddenly, the door opened!

'Oh, Mrs Proudfoot!' said Aunt after only the smallest of hesitations in which she changed her story. 'I thought I might visit.'

'Who are . . . oh, it's you, Jemima Brown!' said Mrs Proudfoot, polite smile turning to a vicious scowl. 'Whatever game are you playing now?' She spotted the constable. 'Don't you dare bring trouble with the law into my household!' She pushed Aunt off the step. Polly stepped forward to catch Aunt, but the constable was there before her, taking a firm hold of the old woman's arm.

'Leave her be!' shouted Polly, running up close. 'Chase me! Go on! I'm the one that took her purse! I'm the thief!'

But the constable ignored Polly, turning his back on her and holding out his free hand, palm upwards, to Aunt. 'Best if you give me whatever it was you took from the gentleman now,' he said. 'It's that, or I'll have to search you.'

Polly looked at Aunt's face, half hidden under the veil, hoping to see clever words in a clever voice come out of her mouth. But Aunt's mouth just twitched. *As if she's going to cry*, thought Polly, shocked. *She's run out of ideas!* Polly watched as Aunt held a fist over the constable's palm, then opened it to drop a pocket watch and a couple of small silver coins into his hand. *So the fishing worked*, thought Polly with a flicker of pride, even as she saw the constable taking the handcuffs from his belt. Aunt's hand was making a tiny shooing away sort of motion, and Polly realised that was a message for her. *No! I'm not going to run and leave you!* She said nothing, but stayed where she was.

'Theft, is it?' said Mrs Proudfoot triumphantly. 'Well, that doesn't surprise me one bit. Miss Brown here owes me rent, so you can add debt to her charges, Constable. You're evicted, Miss Brown, and I'll take what I find down in that basement as payment in lieu.'

'You can't do that!' shouted Polly. 'You'll be the one stealing if you do!' She tried to go down the steps to the basement, but Mrs Proudfoot made a grab to stop her. 'Get off me!'

'It'll be Marshalsea Prison for you, Miss Brown,' said the constable to Aunt.

'That's not fair!' shouted Polly. Everyone knew that Marshalsea was a prison you never got out of. You had to pay for your stay in there, so your debts grew because you could never pay them off. Polly knew that Aunt needed her to do something clever to save them both now, but Polly's mind was so full of fear and fury that she couldn't think in a useful way. But suddenly Aunt could.

'Dibble dabble,' she said, pushing the veil up from her face. 'Dobble pobble!' She opened her gap-toothed mouth into a wide, wonky smile and rolled her eyes at the constable. 'You're ever so handsome, Mr Constable,' she said. 'Shall I kiss you?'

'She's mad,' said the constable, letting go of Aunt's arm and taking a step back.

'I've been saying that for years,' said Mrs Proudfoot. And now Polly did know what to do. She twisted free of Mrs Proudfoot and stepped forward.

'Excuse me,' she said, addressing the constable. 'This lady here is my great-aunt, and she's not right in the head. She needs caring for, she does, not locking away.'

'Huh! Don't you believe that for one minute!' said Mrs Proudfoot.

'But you just said yourself that she's mad,' said Polly. And it seemed that the constable believed it too.

'In that case, the workhouse is probably the best place for you, Miss Brown.' The constable looked at Polly. 'You too, girl, since you're apparently now homeless. We don't want vagrants on the streets upsetting the crowds gathering for Her Majesty's coronation.'

So that summer morning, Polly and Aunt lost their home and everything in it. And they moved to a house as big as a royal palace.

The workhouse.

Chapter 3

St Pancras Workhouse loomed large, filling a length of street that might have fitted twenty houses. It reached back just as far behind the road. It was a building that swallowed into itself people who were in dire trouble, and Polly knew that many of those people who went in never came out again. That thought terrified her.

When the big front door was unlocked with a heavy clunk, and swung open, Polly and Aunt were pushed inside. Polly turned to watch the door being closed, then locked, shutting off freedom and the world as well as the constable. The handcuffs were off Aunt, not needed now there was no hope of escape, and a woman with a big bunch of keys held Aunt's arm, leading her down the corridor. Polly followed. She felt lost and trapped.

'Come along,' said the woman with the keys. That was all Polly could do.

The corridor echoed with sounds of distant wailing and shouts. It smelled of boiled cabbage and something oily. All Polly's life Aunt had used the workhouse as a threat.

'*Keep up with that mizzling, child, and I'll take you to the workhouse myself,*' she'd sometimes said when Polly was small. Or, more lately in hungry times, '*Oh, Poll, they'd have taken me to the workhouse by now if it wasn't for you.*'

Well, now the workhouse had got them both.

Polly hurried forward and held one of Aunt's thin hands in hers. It was shaking. Aunt turned her gaunt face to look at Polly, and gave her a mad sort of a wink that rushed hope into Polly's heart.

'Daft as a brush,' chuckled the woman with the keys as she gestured to a man to take Aunt down another corridor. Her hand slipped from Polly's, and away she went. 'She'll be with her own kind, in the lunatic ward,' said the woman. 'Now, girl, we must get you booked in.'

'Booked?' said Polly. She saw Aunt's little finger wave behind her back, giving Polly a message of hope. 'I can't read a book.' The woman laughed.

'Nobody's asking you to! Your names have to be written into the book,' she said. Polly didn't like that idea. She stood up straight, touched the velvet rose in her hair, and smiled brightly.

'Oh, no thank you very much all the same, ma'am. I was only bringing my aunt here. I'm not staying myself . . .'

'Oh, don't waste your breath in trying that. The constable said you was homeless,' said the woman. 'Come on, this way.'

Polly followed her along more corridors of the strange new place.

'New one for you here, Mr Scrivens, and there's an old woman already been taken into the lunatic ward,' said the woman. She pushed Polly into a room where a balding man stood at a sloping desk. There was a large book open on it, along with a pot of ink and a pen. Mr Scrivens looked at Polly over the top of wire spectacles.

'Name?' he said, turning a page in the book. He picked

up the pen, licked its nib, dipped it into an inkpot, then looked expectantly back at Polly. Polly pushed her hair clear of her eyes, and looked at him, unblinking.

'It's all a mistake, Mr Scrivens, sir.'

'*Use a person's name when you can,*' Aunt always said. '*It makes them feel more obliged to you.*'

'I just need to go home now, thank you, Mr Scrivens,' she said.

'Home?' said Mr Scrivens.

'Yes indeed,' said Polly, opening her eyes big and wide. 'My dear mama will be worried to distraction that I haven't come home yet, and my father will be that angry with anybody that's stolen me, Mr Scrivens, and . . .' Mr Scrivens looked over Polly's head to where she just knew from the look on his face that the woman with the keys must be shaking her head.

'Nope,' said the woman. 'Just look at you, girl. Be sensible now, and give us your name.'

They'd already taken Aunt, taken her home, and taken her things. Polly didn't want to give them anything more of hers, especially if it was going to be scratched into the workhouse book where it would stay forever.

'Sally,' she said. The woman tutted impatiently.

'She's not a Sally. The constable said that their landlady told him she's a Polly.'

'Polly. Surname?' said Mr Scrivens. Polly said nothing.

'The aunt's surname is Brown. She's a Miss Jemima Brown. So this one's likely to be a Polly Brown. Is that right?' Polly nodded. At least she kept her Freeman surname for herself. There was a small satisfaction in that. 'See, Polly?' said the woman. 'There's no point in trying to be tricksy with us. We've seen it all before.'

'Age?' said Mr Scrivens. Polly shrugged.

'Put ten,' said the woman. 'She's thereabouts by the look of her. The old woman claimed to be four and a quarter, but put fifty-five for her.' *Scratch-scratch*, down it all went.

'Oh, and Mr Scrivens,' said the woman. 'The old one also told me that she was Queen of all canary birds, *tweet tweet*. So you can put that down or not as you choose!' She laughed.

'Ah, but that's true,' said Polly. 'And I'm a little sparrow, *tweet tweet!*' She flapped her arms.

'Stop that now,' said Mr Scrivens, scowling as he

shook sand over the book to dry the ink. 'I am not sending you to the lunatic ward to be with your aunt.' He looked up. 'Oakum picking for this one, Mrs Dale. Once she's been deloused of course.'

Polly was taken into a room with a tin bath half full of cold grey water.

'Strip off,' said Mrs Dale. 'Get into that tub there and scrub the dirt off you.'

When a rag and tar soap didn't make Polly as pale as the woman wanted, she scrubbed at Polly with a stiff bristled brush that scoured her skin raw.

'Get off me!' shouted Polly, wriggling away from the brush.

'Black with dirt, you are!' said Mrs Dale.

'I am not!'

'And that hair will have to come off. Just look how thick it is! It's sure to be lousy. Here, I'll take that flower thing out of it.' She yanked Aunt's red rose from Polly's hair.

'Give it back! That's mine!' It was the only thing of her own that Polly still had, and it had hours of Aunt's love and work in the making of it. Polly jumped to try and snatch the rose out of the Mrs Dale's hand, but Mrs Dale held it aloft, then dropped it on to the floor.

The metal shears were cold, slicing with a chomping noise, cropping Polly's hair so close that she could feel a breeze over her scalp. Polly focused on the rose on the floor just out of reach as her hair was taken from her.

'Here, you can put this on.'

The workhouse dress was more shapeless and coarser than her own familiar brown one, which looked a poor ragged thing on the floor. The new dress felt all wrong. For the first time, Polly felt the heat of tears welling in her eyes, but she blinked them away. *'If you're not feeling strong, then just pretend that you are,'* is what Aunt would say. *'Likely you'll soon find your mood catching up with the pretence.'*

There was a white pinafore to go over the dress, and a cap. As Polly bent down to pick the white cap off the floor, she reached over and palmed the red rose into the pinafore's front pocket, and felt a little better. She pulled on the rough cotton cap, grateful that it covered her shorn head, and tied its strings under her chin.

It felt to Polly as if she was dressed to play the part

of somebody else. She put a hand into the pinafore pocket and felt the soft petals of the rose. *I am still Polly Freeman*, she thought. *Aunt loves me, and I love her. But I need to play a part and be clever if Aunt and I are to get out of here.* She smiled brightly.

'Thank you, Mrs Dale, ma'am,' she said, bobbing a curtsy. 'Please can I go to my aunt now?' Mrs Dale didn't even bother to answer that.

'You, girl, are to get to work, or you'll have no meal today.'

The oakum-picking room smelled so powerfully of rank tar that it made Polly gag. Pools of coiled black rope lay on the floor like snakes waiting to pounce. A man with an axe was chopping lengths off a fat rope over a wooden block. *Thwack, chomp.* Children and women sat on stools and benches, each with one of those lengths of black rope on their laps. They were picking at it with fingers and rusty little hooks. Some of the children looked to be only three or four years old, and some of the women were older than Aunt. Their picking fingers were black with tar, and tar was smeared on clothing and faces and hair.

A short little man with a stick came towards Polly.

'New one?' he said. 'Done picking before?' Polly shook her head.

'You'll soon learn. Either that or go hungry.'

The job was to pull apart old rope taken from ships, working the rope back to being tufts of hemp that could be used for caulking the timbers of boats. Mixed with tar, the hemp fibres made a waterproof mash that was poked and hammered between the planks to fill gaps. But ship rope was twisted tight when it was first made, and this used old rope had also been swollen with saltwater, then dried and pulled tight as it held sails and anchors on ships crossing the world's seas. It had oily tar soaked through it. Now it was so tight it was solid. Picking it apart was like trying to pick a tree trunk to shreds. Polly's only tools were her fingers. She tried pinching and pulling at the heavy length of stinking black rope that the axe man placed on her lap. The black-brown tar in it stank, and soon slickly covered her hands and pinafore. She clawed at the hard rope, prying out any tuft she could find, but managed to pull away only a few wisps.

'Hold it between your knees,' said a small voice.

'What?' said Polly.

A skinny, pale girl sitting on a low stool opposite Polly was steadily watching her, even as her own fingers kept picking fast at her length of rope. Polly saw that the pile of oakum on the floor in front of the pale girl was bigger than the piles in front of anyone else. The girl gave Polly a quick little smile.

'Keep picking,' she whispered, 'or . . .'

Thwack! The man's stick hit the ground at Polly's feet, but she'd felt the wind of it passing close by her face, and she jumped.

'No idling!' said the man.

'I . . .'

'And no answering back neither. It's half rations for you 'til you learn some respect.' He pinned a small red rag to the shoulder of Polly's dress. 'So they'll know to give you half rations.' The woman picking at rope next to Polly sniggered as if the man had told a good joke.

'I was only telling her how it's done,' said the girl on the stool. 'How's she to know if nobody shows her?'

'That's it,' said Polly. 'I shouldn't even be here, by rights.' The women and children all turned to listen to somebody answering back when she'd just been warned not to. They kept on picking as they listened and watched. Polly sat up straighter and tilted her head back. 'Where I come from it's the servants what do the dirty sorts of work while I'm playing my piano or eating little cakes and that.'

'Give over!' said a toothless woman. 'You're no better than the rest of us.'

'Look at my hands,' said Polly, holding them out in a way that felt daring because it meant she stopped picking. 'Until I touched the rope here these hands were clean enough to handle the queen's best white undergarments.'

They laughed at that as they pick, pick, picked. Everybody's hands were black with tar. It was nice, making them all laugh. Polly felt less of an outsider already.

'My own father was a prince, you know,' she said.

'Oh yeah? And I'm the May Queen!' laughed a scrawny woman as she bent to pick up another length of rope. 'So how come you've you ended up along with the rest of us here, then, Your Royal Highness?'

'Hard times,' said Polly, and her audience shrugged

and turned back to the work on their laps. They all of them knew about hard times.

'Less jabbering, more picking,' said the man, nodding towards the few wisps of hemp on the floor in front of Polly that was all she'd managed to pick so far.

Polly's thoughts turned to Aunt. Were they making her work like this over in the lunatic ward? Was she telling stories? Had they dressed her in different clothes? They must have taken the grand black dress with its flowers down the front from her. Polly shifted the rope on her lap, making sure it wasn't crushing the red rose hidden in her pocket.

Polly was well used to doing hours of stitching, but she and Aunt would get up and stretch every so often. Or they'd rub the aching part on each other's backs and shoulders to ease them. Stopping work, even for a moment, wasn't allowed here. Polly's back soon hurt deeply from the constant bending over. Her fingertips, rubbed raw, screamed with the pain of pulling at the hard hemp, and her head ached from the smell of tar. The chat around her quietened as the hours went on, pick, pick, picking.

When one old woman went to use the pot in the corner, there was a scuffle of those who could reach to steal tufts from her oakum pile to add to their own. Polly watched. The old woman either didn't notice that her oakum had been taken, or she was used to it happening. She simply sat down and carried on as if nothing had changed. Polly's pile was still by far the smallest. Should she steal from others to add to it? Pick, pick, pick.

There was a knack to picking and then twisting to get the most out of each pick. Polly found that she was getting better and faster at it even as her fingers got increasingly fiery-raw and sore.

When the bell rang to mark the end of the working day there was a common sigh of relief around her as people dropped the ropes on to the floor and straightened up. Polly rolled her shoulders and moved her head from side to side to ease her cramped muscles.

'Not too bad. For royalty, anyway,' said the man, nudging Polly's pile of oakum with a foot. 'I'll make it full rations today after all. Keep going like that, and you'll do all right.' He unpinned the red rag.

Polly looked down to the floor, surprised at the

praise, and saw that her pile of rope pickings was bigger than she remembered. And the oakum pile in front of the stool opposite her was smaller now than some of the other piles.

'Oh!'

The girl who'd been sitting on the stool was already standing, lining up with the other children and women beside the wall. *She gave me some from her own pile*, Polly realised. The kindness of that gift relaxed Polly's insides into a sort of internal smile.

'Thank you!' she whispered as she went to stand behind the girl. The girl gave a little waggle of her head to show that she'd heard, but she didn't turn around or say anything as they waited in line. Polly saw now that others were watching the two of them, and the girl didn't seem to want to draw attention. Was that how you survived in here, by quietly getting work done and not getting noticed? Perhaps claiming to be royal had been a mistake? The looks coming her way from some of the other girls certainly weren't friendly.

The workhouse inmates ate in the biggest room Polly had ever seen. It was a great, high echoey space with long lines of tables and benches. Polly queued with the other children, all of them holding bowls as they shuffled towards a huge, steaming pot where a man with a ladle slopped something into each bowl. From the smell of it, Polly guessed the grey slop was a sort of porridge. She slid her way along the bench, looking around as she sat down. The adult men inmates must eat at a different time, she thought. But were people from the lunatic ward in here? Polly recognised one or two faces of people who'd lived in her neighbourhood. Two boys whose parents and brothers had died. A girl who'd worked as a maid until she fell down the stairs and broke her leg. But most of the people were strangers to her. She looked up and down, searching for Aunt's white hair and beaky nose. But the older women at the long tables all looked the same at a distance, and none of them looked like Aunt.

The overseer stepped on to the platform at one side of the room.

'Thanks be to God for the good food that the Christian charity of the council gives us,' he bellowed. The 'amen' that followed got hidden by the sound of spoons clattering into bowls.

Polly quickly spooned up all her grey sloppy gruel, wiping the bowl with a finger to get the last smear of it. It didn't taste good, but eating had woken her stomach and made her realise how very hungry she was for anything to fill it. She remembered the threat of half rations if she didn't pick enough oakum. Her red-raw fingertips stung as she licked them. They tasted of tar. But she must keep picking or she'd go hungry. *That's how they get the work out of you*, she thought. *By threatening to starve you.* A boy with a withered arm sat opposite Polly, and she saw that his bowl had less food in it. He was as gaunt as a twig. Hunger was a powerful master. She looked, but she couldn't see where the kind girl was now. *I want to tell Aunt about her*, she thought.

As they left the dining hall, Polly still couldn't see the girl. She began to wonder if she'd made her up like a story, to make herself feel better? Polly was so tired that the world seemed to sway around her, and she didn't feel sure of anything other than an ache in her heart for Aunt, shut somewhere else in that huge place full of hundreds of strange people.

Polly staggered after the other girls into a big room full of square wooden beds. There seemed to be three girls to each bed, and no place to spare. Polly just stood there until somebody called over to her.

'Oi, you.' It was an older girl. Mrs Dale had told the girl earlier to show the new girl where to go and what to do, but until now she hadn't even spoken to Polly. Now she pointed to a bed on the far side of the room. 'You share over there with Min. She's had that bed to herself since Dora died and Mary moved into mine.' The other girls nearby looked at Polly, and one of them giggled, a hand to her mouth.

'Why's that funny?' said Polly.

'Nobody wants to share with Min,' said the giggling girl between snorts of laughter. 'She's got the cough that did for Dora. But that bed's the only one with a space, so you've no choice about it. You go there.' Giggle, giggle.

Polly looked over to the bed, and saw with a flip of her heart that Min was the kind girl who had helped her. She was real! Polly was so exhausted, so glad of the friendly face, that she ignored the warnings about deadly coughs. She walked over to the bed with Min in it. Min's pale face framed by her white cotton cap smiled up at Polly, and she moved to one side of the bed, making room.

When Polly hung her pinafore from a wall peg, she put her hand into the pocket and took out the red rose, hidden within her fist, as she lifted the blanket and lay down beside Min.

'This is for you,' whispered Polly. 'Look.' She held up the blanket, making a cave in which the two of them could see the red rose in the slight, wavering light from the candle on the far side of the room.

'Oh!' said Min. 'That's . . . oh, it's . . .!' She reached out to touch a thin finger to one petal. 'What is it?'

'It's a rose,' said Polly. 'A flower. Not a real one. My aunt made it. You can have it if you like.'

'No, I can't!' whispered Min. 'It's . . . it's too good. You must keep it. If you let me see it sometimes, that's enough. But take care, 'cos . . .'

'Silence!' bellowed the voice of Mrs Dale suddenly, making them both jump.

The candles were snuffed, and all went dark. Polly reached out to put the rose back into her pinafore pocket.

Then she lay curled on the lumpy, smelly straw mattress and closed her eyes. She was glad to have a friend, glad to be resting, but she worried about Aunt.

Min coughed. Polly slept.

Chapter 4

A clanging bell shocked Polly awake, making her wonder where she was. Then she remembered. She was in the workhouse, along with a roomful of other girls, and one of them was in the bed beside her. Min. But somebody else, she realised, was standing behind their bed, and she was reaching a hand into Polly's pinafore pocket.

'Hey, get out of there!' shouted Polly, scrambling up to grab the thieving girl's sleeve. But the big, bold girl had the red rose in her hand. She raised it high to wave at the others, who were sitting up in beds now, rubbing their eyes and yawning.

'See this?' she shouted. 'Ever so fancy! I think I'll have it.' She laughed, holding the red rose against her tangle of brown hair.

'It's mine! Give it back!' Polly launched herself at the girl, trying to snatch the rose without crushing its petals. She took a firm hold of the girl's wrist in both of her hands, squeezing tight. 'Give it back now!' she shouted.

But the girl had allies, and they grabbed at Polly, pulling her away.

'Just what do you think you're doing?' Mrs Dale stomped into the room. 'Leave that new girl alone!'

'But she was stealing, missis.'

'I was not!' shouted Polly. '*You* were!'

'Look!' The thieving girl held up the rose. 'She was trying to steal this off of me, Mrs Dale! Wasn't she?' The girl looked about, and other girls nodded and said it was true.

'That's a lie . . .!' began Polly. Then she saw Min, kneeling up on their bed and giving her a bit of a warning look and a little shake of the head. So Polly stopped her complaint. She went still and quiet, and in moments the room filled with the clatter of girls getting up. But that big girl still had her rose. Polly was tight with miserable fury as she got dressed.

As they queued outside to wash at the pump, Min leaned towards Polly and whispered, 'I've got it hidden.'

'What? The rose?'

'Shh,' warned Min, glancing around to make sure they weren't being overheard. 'Yeah. It's in a corner of the bed straw. It isn't squashed.'

'How . . .?'

Min smiled at Polly's astonished face. 'She'd put it under her bedcover. I just shoved it into the bed straw.'

'In their bed?' whispered Polly. 'Won't . . .'

'Nah,' said Min. 'They'll never think we'd hide it in their bed. It's safe.'

'What are you whispering with her about?' asked one of the bigger girls.

'Min was saying that exnepiplobing is frool in here,' said Polly with a raise of her eyebrows and a steady stare at the girl. Not knowing how to answer that, the girl quickly got back into line to mutter with her friends.

'What did that mean?' said Min.

'Nothing,' said Polly. 'My aunt says if you get caught in a tight corner, say something that sounds clever and sure, and half of people will go away rather than admit they don't understand it.' Min laughed. She was pretty when she smiled. Then the laugh turned into a cough.

As they sat picking at ropes again, Polly hated the high walls boxing them in, the smell, the sore-fingered work, and the not knowing how Aunt was. She asked Min, 'How can we get out of here?'

'We can't,' said Min. 'Nobody does. Not unless they've got somebody on the outside who comes to get you. Or a job you get taken away for. Chimney sweep or skivvy perhaps.'

'Aunt's the only family I've got,' said Polly. 'She needs me to get *her* out.' Pick, pick. 'But I can't stay here.'

'Why not?' said Min.

Polly looked at the hunched figures around her, heads down, pick, pick, picking. They were all pale, some coughing, lots of them with fewer teeth than Aunt. They mostly looked as if they wouldn't run outside even if the door was opened wide. The thought of turning into one of them terrified her. Yet she could see exactly how hunger and tedium could make you into a person who wasn't a full person any more.

'I want to sew flowers again. I want to laugh with my

aunt,' said Polly. 'I want . . . oh, all sorts.' She looked at Min, head down, picking fast. 'And I don't want Aunt to die. She always said that she would, if she had to go into a workhouse. If Aunt died, I'd have nobody.' Pick, pick, pick. 'How long have you been in this place, Min?' Pick, pick, pick.

'Just about forever,' said Min. 'My dad brought me in when I was so little he was carrying me.' She stopped picking. 'I remember his hands, big and strong, holding me to him. I remember the smell of his shoulder that I had my nose squashed against.' She did a little shrug. 'He said he'd come back for me, but he never did.'

'Have you tried to get out and find him?' said Polly. Pick, pick, pick.

'How could I?' said Min. She was quiet for a moment, thinking. 'They say if I'm lucky I'll be taken as a skivvy in a year or two. I'd like that, being in a real house.'

Polly looked at small, delicate Min. She couldn't imagine her carrying buckets of coal up and down stairs. Maybe she could learn how to sew shirt pieces? Or even embroider flowers. *But had Min ever seen flowers?* Polly wondered.

'If you got out of here, you could see so much, and . . . well, you'd be free,' said Polly. Pick, pick, pick. 'You might be hungry sometimes, but there's usually things you can do to get by. I'm getting out of here as soon as I can.' Pick, pick, pick.

'What will you do when you get out?' said Min.

Polly stopped picking. 'I want to be a dressmaker, cutting and stitching and shaping to make beautiful clothes. Clothes not just to keep people warm and looking nice. I want to make clothes that make people . . . well, happy, I suppose.' She looked down at the tar-stained pinafore over the rough brown dress she was wearing. 'I'd put birds and flowers and pictures, just tiny, maybe, so that only the person wearing them knows that their clothes are special.' Polly looked at Min, who hadn't stopped picking. 'Wouldn't you like a dress that's special, just for you, instead of belonging to the workhouse?'

'Mm. That sounds nice,' said Min. She had a slight smile on her face that made Polly feel happy and sad at the same time. She realised that Min had never thought of such a thing as owning her own clothes.

'We will get out of here, you know,' said Polly. Pick, pick, pick.

But days passed and Polly couldn't see any way to escape. Doors were always locked. Inmates were always watched. *'Just stay alert like a sparrow for the moment when somebody drops a crumb,'* said Aunt in Polly's head. So Polly watched and waited, eyes and ears alert for a crumb of a chance. She'd got the rose back, ready to take out with her. She'd pulled threads in her dress loose, under her pinafore where they wouldn't show, and the rose was tied there.

Min found an old nail for Polly to use for picking the oakum. That made picking faster, so Polly worried less about whether or not she'd get full rations to eat. The oakum piles grew, were taken away, made again, taken away again, on and on. The hours and days passed with Polly repeating the actions as if she was a machine. But Min seemed to know that Polly hadn't given up.

'When you get out of here, what'll your house be like?' whispered Min one day. She gave Polly a small, lopsided grin that showed this was a game. 'If you could have any one of all them houses out there.' She nodded up at the high window. Pick, pick, pick.

'I'll have one with no landlord or landlady,' said Polly. 'It'll belong proper to Aunt and me. It'll have a good hot stove to cook on and keep warm by. Lots of coal to feed it. A chair each to sit on, with cushions. Windows clean and low enough to see out of properly, letting light in. A soft bed with plenty of covers. The top cover will be embroidered with every different flower and leaf and butterfly there is.'

'What'll you eat?' asked Min. Pick, pick, pick.

'Peaches,' said Polly.

'What's that?'

'A bit like an apple, but soft and sort of fluffy and orangey-pink, and so juicy sweet you can't hardly believe it. I found one once that had rolled off a market table. I reckon it was the best taste in all of London.'

'What'll you wear?' whispered Min.

'Something as red as a robin's chest,' said Polly. 'With birds sewn on to it. Flying birds. A yellow canary. A white swan.'

'What's one of them?' asked Min, and Polly tried to describe the power and beauty and strangeness of the white bird as big as an angel.

'You'll see one someday,' said Polly.

'Will I?' said Min.

'Yeah,' said Polly. 'I'll show you them on the river. You're coming out of here with me.' Min's lopsided smile grew wide.

'Truly?' Pick, pick, pick went Min even faster. 'But have you thought how we can get out?' Polly had no ideas yet, but didn't want to disappoint Min. She leaned close.

'I expect Mr Scrivens will call for a golden coach to take us away if I just ask him nicely and tell him my dad's a prince,' she said. Min giggled.

'You're not truly royal are you, Polly?'

'Well, Aunt does say that my dad was "a man of royal blood".' Polly shrugged. 'But other times she says he was "the lowest of the low of all mankind", so what she says makes about as much sense as a snake buying itself a pair of boots. You know she's in the lunatic ward, don't you?' Polly glanced at Min, waiting for her to laugh about that. But Min didn't.

'Poor her,' said Min as they both went on picking. 'I should think it's frightening in there.' She bent down to neaten her pile of oakum on the floor. She looked up sideways at Polly, her grey-green eyes earnest. 'Truly, Polly, how could you and me ever get out of here?'

'Perhaps we can dress in women's gowns from the laundry, and just walk out?' said Polly.

'We're too small to look like grown women,' said Min. 'We'd do better pretending to be boys.'

'That's an idea!' said Polly, picking faster and suddenly seeing a real possibility in her mind.

'When we get out,' said Min, 'we could thieve something, and make sure to get caught.'

'What, and get shut away again? No thanks!' said Polly.

'But don't you see?' said Min. 'If we thieve, they'll send us to that Botany Bay place ever so far away in another country. Then we could make a home there. I'd like to go on a boat. I've never seen the sea. I might see swans then.'

For days Polly watched and tried to think of a way to get hold of boys' clothing. She'd quickly bent down and picked up a cap dropped by a boy, shoving it under her dress and clamping it under an arm. *That's one crumb pecked up*, she thought . . . until the boy said, 'Hey, give that back,' and she did. Could she get into the boys' dormitory, or perhaps the laundry? She watched and waited for chances, and tried to make chances too.

'Please, mister,' said Polly to the overseer. 'I can sew better than most, so can't I be put in the sewing room?' There might be boys' clothes to make or mend there. But the overseer didn't even answer her.

'I've been thinking too,' whispered Min in their bed in the dark. 'We could get ourselves an injury bad enough to have to go to the infirmary. I was in there once when I was sick and fainted. They leave you lying there with nobody watching. And there's windows we could get out of if we climb up.'

'How could we both get injured at the same time, though?' said Polly. She remembered the threats of contagion from Min that the other girls had made when she first came into the workhouse. Min's cough was bad, but not bad enough to stop her working. 'Perhaps we could use your picking nail to poke holes in our skin to look like scarlet-fever spots.'

But then something happened that changed their plans completely.

Chapter 5

As they sat at the long tables, waiting for the overseer to shout out thanks to God for the splat of grey food in the bowls in front of them, Polly saw there was somebody with the usual man with the stick.

'That's the parish officer, that is,' whispered Min. 'I've seen him before.'

The parish officer wore a splendid blue coat with red and gold trimmings. He rocked back on his heels, his thumbs wedged behind the thick leather belt around his plump waist. He tipped back his rather square head, and he bellowed to the room, 'Your attention, please, St Pancras Workhouse inmates! I have an announcement to make.' He paused, waiting for all eyes to be on him before her continued. 'An exceptionally excellent opportunity has arisen for some of you here to learn a trade and secure a respectable living.' A murmur of interest swelled around the room. 'But this applies only to persons aged between nine and twelve years old.'

'That's us!' whispered Min.

'A mill in Nottingham is in need of strong child workers, and is offering apprenticeships.' The officer looked directly towards the long table where Polly and Min sat with the other oakum-picking girls. 'I'm told,' said the parish officer, 'that when you get to this place of work you will find that roast beef is eaten most days. Plum pudding was mentioned too for those who work hard. Rides in your master's carriage and all sorts of treats and riches could also be yours.' Polly squeezed Min's thin hand under the table. 'What is more, those chosen children will be given an education in return for their work. What do you think of that?'

Polly's mouth opened to ask a whole lot of questions, but Min shushed her with a warning nudge before any sound came out.

The parish officer went on. 'Those chosen will be

leaving here the day after tomorrow. I already have a list of likely names kindly provided for me by Mr Scrivens. Those on the list will be summoned to his office this afternoon to be looked over, then chosen or otherwise.'

The parish officer was a short man, but very aware of the plumage of his uniform. He set his shoulders back once more. 'Tomorrow, our country crowns our new monarch, Queen Victoria, to gloriously reign over us. For you children venturing northwards to serve our blessed country in your own small way, representing the parish of St Pancras in another part of Her Majesty's kingdom . . . er, queendom . . . will be a signal honour. Hurrah for Her Majesty!'

'Hurrah,' muttered the workhouse inmates not nearly as enthusiastically.

The moment the parish officer and overseer had stepped down from the platform, a surge of sound swelled through the hall as people turned to each other.

'I don't want to leave me mam.'

'Roast beef, did he say?'

'How far away is the north?'

Polly looked at Min and pulled an agonised a face.

'What about Aunt? He said only children are wanted.'

'You need to ask her what to do,' said Min.

So, as they filed out of the dining hall, Polly broke ranks with the other girls and hurried down a corridor towards the lunatic ward.

'And where do you think you're going?' asked an orderly.

'Urgent message for someone in the lunatic ward. From Mr Scrivens,' said Polly. '*Believe in what you're saying, say it boldly, and others will believe it too,*' said Aunt in her head. 'It's very urgent, Mr Scrivens said.'

The man waved her on. 'Be quick about it then.'

Polly only just recognised the woman in a drab black dress, with a plain cream cap tied under her chin. All the women in the room were dressed in the same way. One sat rocking herself back and forth on a bench, another crouched on the floor, hands over her head. Polly saw that that one woman's hands were bound together with rope as if she was a criminal. Aunt looked sane and proper, although she was singing a strange lilting tune as she knitted a square of knobbly thick cream cotton yarn.

Polly's heart swelled, and she smiled as she recognised that the song that Aunt was singing was Polly's daddy's song.

'*Olele, olele moliba makasi*

Olele Mboka na ye, mboka, mboka kasai-i.'

A nurse caught Polly's eye, then nodded towards Aunt. 'It's a daft, mad sort of a song but it does seem to soothe the others,' she said.

'She's my great-aunt Jem,' said Polly proudly. Aunt stopped singing, and turned at the sound of Polly's voice.

'Oh!' she said. 'It's my little sparrow!' She reached up to touch Polly's cheek. 'Are they caring for you, Poll?' That was what Polly wanted to know about Aunt. But she could already see something of the answer to that question. In spite of the company she was in, Aunt looked content.

'Aunt,' said Polly, crouching down to be face to face with her. 'There's a chance I might be able to go and be apprenticed.'

'Oh my,' said Aunt, clasping her hands together. 'Just what I've always hoped for you!' Then her smile slipped. 'But Polly, we don't have the money for it.'

'I know,' said Polly. 'But that's the thing. They want us at a mill, and we don't even have to pay. But it's in Nottingham, a long way away. And they only want children, so you couldn't come with us. What d'you think?'

The nurse was watching and listening. Polly leaned closer to Aunt, whispering now. 'I'd have to leave you here, Aunt, and . . .'

Aunt patted her arm. 'Don't you fret about me, Pol. I can look after myself. You know that. I may be knitting dishcloths in an asylum, but in my head I'm off all over, visiting the places I've known in my life. This suits me very well for now. And to think of you being apprenticed and learning a trade somewhere away from here makes me happy.'

'Time you went back to your own ward,' the nurse told Polly.

'Can I just . . .?'

'Bibble babble,' interrupted Aunt. She stood up from her chair, held her skirts and did a little dance. 'Bobble bodkins!'

'Aunt . . .' began Polly. She knew very well this was

Aunt playing madness, but why, just when Polly had to go?

'Woopsy!' Aunt tipped over in her mad dance so that she had to catch hold of Polly, giving her a brief firm bony hug as Polly righted Aunt, hugging her back. 'Go, my love,' whispered Aunt urgently. 'Fly free, little sparrow. Go.'

'I'll come back for you,' said Polly. 'I promise.'

Chapter 6

Polly looked left and right at the other children lined up with her for inspection by the parish officer. Which of them looked the strongest? Next to Polly, Min's pinched face was concentrating on holding in the coughs that so often took over her body. The other children mostly looked as pale as Min did, the skin on their faces tight to their skull bones. Polly turned to Min:

'Think yourself strong, then that's what they'll see.' Aunt always said that belief was a catching kind of a thing.

She was right, because Polly Brown and Min Ogden were both put on the list to go.

Two days later, they left St Pancras Workhouse. They

were scrubbed as clean as they could be, although Polly's and Min's hands remained black from the rope tar. The children were given new shawls and jackets and caps. Lined up in the corridor, Polly waited, heart beating fast, for the door to open to the outside world.

'Ain't we grand!' said Min, knotting her shawl ends. 'Have you got the . . .'

'Yeah. In my pinny pocket,' said Polly, patting where the rose was. She could take the rose with her, but leaving Aunt behind made her ache with sadness. *Do you really want me to go, Aunt?* thought Polly. *Or are you playing a part to make me feel better?* Either way, the best way to free Aunt was to make a success of her apprenticeship fast, then come back in triumph to claim her.

'Line up, two by two, smallest at the front, biggest at the back,' ordered Mr Scrivens.

They shuffled to sort themselves. Then the door opened, and Polly pushed forward, clutching Min's sleeve to take her through the doorway with her.

'Oi, no shoving or I'll keep you back!' shouted Mr Scrivens.

But Polly was out.

She was out into sounds of rumbling wheels and clopping horses, shouting people, laughter, and a big, high blue sky above. There was cheering from a small crowd gathered near the workhouse entrance. On the road were two carts with a pair of big horses hitched to each of them. Parish beadles in smart tailcoats with brass buttons stood either side to clear a path leading to the wagons. They stood stiff and straight, holding long sticks. Polly saw that they were sweating in their thick woollen uniforms in the June sunshine. She couldn't quite believe such formality and fuss being made over workhouse children.

Some of the crowd were passers-by, stopping to see what was going on. But others were families of children who were going. They were shouting out names, and waving. Some pushing. Some crying. Polly realised that the beadle's sticks were to keep those people back from the children.

'He's *my* boy! Mine! Don't you take him from me!'

'Come on,' Min urged Polly, pulling her to the front so they were the first to reach a cart, climbing up on to the clean straw. Perhaps it was better not to have anybody to leave. Apart from Aunt.

'This is like a nest!' said Polly, settling herself down. Aunt would have liked knowing there was a nest for her sparrow, she thought. She looked to the workhouse windows that dazzled with sunshine, hiding any faces looking out. Might Aunt be watching? Polly smiled brightly and waved, just in case. *I love you*, she thought fiercely.

The parish officer made a great show of handing each child a piece of gingerbread and a silver shilling. Polly wondered why. Then she saw three top-hatted gentlemen smilingly watching the excited children waving their gifts for everyone to see. '*People will pay to make a display of being generous.*' Like those shopkeepers who gave Aunt things when they thought she was rich and if others were watching.

'Cor!' said Min, taking a bite of her gingerbread, then coughing on the crumbs.

Polly sniffed the gingery sweetness of her own chunk of dry cake, then slipped it into one of her pinafore pockets for later. She put the shilling deep into the other pocket, along with the rose. Then, with a sudden jerk, the cart lumbered into motion. *Clip clop*, they were off amid excited chatter and shouted goodbyes and good lucks, and some crying.

Polly looked around, the sunshine making her squint after having been indoors for so long. Riding high, they had a good view, passing shops and houses and churches.

'You were right about being outside,' said Min. But she clutched tight to the side of the cart, watching the only home she could remember until the workhouse was out of sight. Polly felt thin Min quivering as if she was cold.

'Finish your gingerbread,' said Polly. 'It'll stop you feeling sick from the jolting. You can share mine later.' She didn't feel hungry herself. She felt full of a thick mix of hope and sadness and excitement. Then she looked at Min's face and laughed.

Min had never travelled on wheels before. She kept leaning over the side to watch in wonder as they went round.

It was the colours that Polly noticed most on the journey north. Bright blue skies with small puffs of white cloud. Flowers and weeds in yellows and reds and oranges. Vivid green fields and tree leaves. She noticed sounds too. The ongoing rumble and clop and clatter of the cart. If the cart stopped, she could hear birdsong, or the clang of a blacksmith's hammer on iron, the moo of a cow, the bubbling of a stream. She thought of Aunt, shut in that dreary place of dull non-colours and cabbage and tar smells, and sounds of wailing and keys turning in locks.

'Taste that air,' said Polly to Min when they got out into the countryside. Min opened her mouth and sucked in air, then frowned.

'What does it taste of?' she said.

'Nothing at all,' beamed Polly. That nothing was as refreshing as spring water after the constant taste of tar in the air of the oakum room, and the smoky, smoggy air of London.

At first the children in the carts sang and teased each other and threw straw and laughed. As the first day wore on they became quieter.

It took three days and two nights for the carts to get to the mill. By then most of the children had spent their shillings in the towns and villages they'd stopped in on the way, buying such treats as sticks of sour rhubarb with paper twists of sugar to dip them into. Polly looked longingly at them, but she liked even more the feeling of that shilling, still with its spending potential intact, in her pocket.

'*Having money in life gives you choices,*' is what Aunt said. Polly wanted choices. Min had never in her life been offered choices. She'd never had even a farthing of her own. Now she spent her shilling on buns and a length of silky blue ribbon that she tied in her hair. She shared the buns with Polly.

Min's cough got bad on the journey. They were all sore and stiff from sitting and lying down and leaning in the straw that got more squashed and dirty by the day as the carts lurched and bumped and rumbled along. The children slept in the carts while the carters went into inns for the nights, taking a big leather bag with him. It must have money in it, thought Polly. There was a big, old tarpaulin to pull over each of the carts at night, making a fug of warmth from the bodies beneath. But then rain came, and Min shivered all the time in spite of her new shawl.

'Good hot roast beef soon,' Polly reminded her.

It was still raining as they travelled through the streets of Nottingham to arrive at the big, blackened brick building that growled and reeked of an oily smell. They came into a yard where huge grey bales of cotton were being unloaded from a wagon.

'Look sharp,' said the carter over his shoulder to the children. 'This is it.'

'It' wasn't at all what Polly had expected. And she saw something that made a cold finger of fear run down her back.

'Look there,' she said to Min.

A row of filthy children in ragged clothes were shuffling along, herded between buildings by a man with a heavy truncheon. He halted those children in the rainy yard, and came across to speak to the carter. The hollow-eyed mill children looked up at the London children in the carts. They didn't smile. They didn't talk. And the London children were silent now too, watching back. Polly felt Min trembling beside her.

'It's worse,' whispered Min, and Polly knew she meant worse than the workhouse.

Polly leaned over the cart side to hear the carter talking to the man from the mill.

'Two guineas each for twenty of them is what I was told,' said the Nottingham man in an accent that was strange to Polly.

'That's it,' said the carter. 'Forty guineas. I have it here.' He patted the leather bag slung over his body. 'I was sent with twenty-two children in case of wastage along the way. but none have fallen ill or run away so I still have them all. Can you take the extra two?'

The mill man shook his head of glistening wet hair. 'Not without the master's approval, I can't. And he's away now. On his honeymoon in Italy.'

'Ooh, very nice!' laughed the carter.

'All right for some, eh?' said the man. 'So I can't help you with those two extra.'

'Fair enough,' said the carter. 'I'm travelling on to the Greg's Quarry Bank Mill to collect an order of calico. Maybe they can make use of them there.'

'Those'll be the lucky ones then. They're soft on apprentices at Quarry Bank, I've heard. Right, get them all down and I'll take a look at what you've got for us.'

'Hold back,' whispered Polly to Min.

'Why?'

Polly just put a hand on Min's arm as the others from both carts climbed down to stand in the rain, watched by the silent mill children. The carter was counting them as they got in line.

'. . . nineteen, twenty. That's it. Let's get the deal done inside, out of the rain, eh?' Polly was beginning to sit back when she heard something that made her hold her breath.

'Unless,' said the Nottingham man, 'those other two children are stronger than any of these ones? Where are they?'

'Oi, you two!' The carter slapped the side of the cart. 'Get down here quick sharp!'

'Cough, Min,' said Polly as the two of them slid over the straw, then down from the cart on to the wet yard to stand beside the others.

Cough! went Min. Having started coughing, Min was bent double with real coughs that shook her whole body. Polly coughed too, but faking it. Then, as the men stepped towards them, Polly bit hard on her lip, tasting the salty sour taste of her own blood bleeding, and she coughed it out, bright red, on to her hand. The Nottingham man took a step back.

'No thank you!' he said. 'I'm not taking those two! I thought you said they were all healthy?' He looked at the carter in disgust. 'Get them back in that cart. The rest of you, get inside.'

Polly helped Min back on to the cart and made a sort of cave out of the sheet of smelly tarpaulin. They pulled the squashed straw around themselves for warmth as the drizzle continued and the light outside dimmed. Polly's lip throbbed, but she didn't care.

After a time, the carter came out to them with hunks of hard bread and bowls of broth.

'You two are to stay on the cart overnight,' he said. 'They won't have you in with the other children for fear of infection.' He grinned a nod towards Polly. 'I saw you biting your lip. Crafty. I can't say I blame you. This isn't a place I'd choose to stay. I'm sorry to leave any of them here. Not my choice, of course.' Then he was gone.

'We could run away,' said Min.

'Mm,' said Polly. But she didn't move. Min was

coughing. It was wet and cold out there, and their nest in the straw was relatively warm. Besides, where would they go? 'That man said they're good to apprentices at Quarry Bank,' she said. 'If we've a chance of them taking us on, we can earn money, learn a trade, then fetch Aunt out of the workhouse. We could set up in a house of our own. Do you fancy having a cat? Aunt and I had a big ginger one once. He was called Mangle. But the horrible woman upstairs fed him meat scraps so he went to live with her and got called Parkin instead. Shall we have a garden so we could grow spuds and cabbages to eat? Flowers too?'

But Min was asleep.

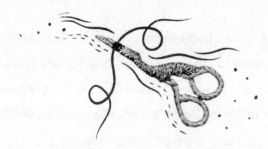

Chapter 7

The other cart set off back to London, but the cart Polly and Min were in trundled on into new country for another two days.

'Heading westwards now,' said the carter.

The sky cleared, and the carter, either liking to have company or being kind, let the two girls sit on the driving seat with him now. They had the steady pair of horses' rumps in front of them, tails twitching as their great strong haunches powered along, strong necks nodding with bouncing manes of black hair, pointed ears twitching. One of the horses had two brown ears, one had one brown and one white. *That one's mine, and the other one is Min's*, thought Polly, and added a stable to her imaginary home of the future. The landscape got hillier and wilder, the villages and inns further apart.

'Where are the people?' asked Min, looking around at the high, rocky landscape with hardly a tree or building in it.

'Just think what this place must be like in winter,' said the carter. 'Bleak as an empty plate when you're hungry. Give me London any day.' But Polly liked the space and the clean air.

They came to Manchester where buildings crowded around them again, and the air was thick with noise and smoke and smells. There were grand houses, chapels and churches and civic buildings, but also rows and rows of joined-together brick houses. A waterwheel seemed to churn the river on the side of a tall, brick-built factory.

'Is that Quarry Bank Mill?' said Polly. But it wasn't.

They drove right through Manchester and out the other side into green again. Through a village of brick-built homes with steps up to front doors and railings in front, then down a track, past a big brick house, then a glimpse of a grander house the orange colour of some cheese, until finally . . .

'Flippin boggits, it's . . .!' Min held out her arms as wide as she could reach. The vast brick building had almost as much window as wall. 'Five layers of windows!' she said, counting on her fingers. Both girls put hands over their ears as the place roared powerfully loudly as they came close. 'What is that noise?' asked Min.

'Steady now,' said the carter to the two horses as their hooves slid and clopped down the cobbled hill towards where the mill sat in the valley bottom. Then he turned to Min and shouted over the noise. 'It's the wheel winding all the machines that are inside the mill. Biggest waterwheel in the world, I was told. Powers hundreds of machines.' The carter shook his head.

'Why?' said Min.

'To make cloth,' said the carter. 'Cotton fluff is grown and brought here from over an ocean, then spun and worked into cloth for me to take to London to be sewn into sheets. Do you suppose the people sleeping in those sheets ever think of the work done by so many to make them? I know I never did 'til I saw the mills in action.'

Polly clutched the seat edge as the cart halted in the shadow of that huge building full of workers and machines. For a moment the three of them sat there, swamped by sounds and thoughts, and by the strange sensation of being still after so much travelling. It made Polly jump when a dark-haired man in a frock coat suddenly popped up beside their wagon seat. The carter doffed his hat to the man.

'Good day to you, sir. I'm from St Pancras, London, sir. To collect an order of calico. But I also have two likely apprentice girls if you can use them? They've been cleared as fit and suitable for mill work but were surplus to what was needed at Murkitt's Mill.'

'Draw up over there, then come inside and we can sort the business,' said the man. 'Leave the girls in the cart for now.'

Polly and Min looked at each other, sharing the unspoken question; should they make a run for it? The great mill had a power that scared Polly, but it excited her too.

'Let's see what it's like inside, then decide if we want to stay,' she said.

'They might not want us,' said Min, pale-faced.

'Slap your cheeks like this,' said Polly, slapping her

own. 'It puts colour in them and makes you look more healthy.'

After a while they were beckoned down from the cart.

'This way,' said a man with a red face and scrubbing-brush side whiskers.

Polly jumped down from the cart seat, and Min followed.

'Are we to stay, sir?' asked Min.

'That depends,' said the man. 'You've come on a day when Dr Holland is doing his checks here, so he can take a look and see if you're strong enough for the work. I'm told he's up at the house now, so we can catch him there.' The man pointed back up the steep track they'd driven down. Polly and Min followed him up the cobbled lane to the big brick house they'd passed by earlier. It had large windows, and a porch over the door. Beside the house was a garden with beans growing up sticks, marrows, marigold flowers and more. There were sheds for privies and washing. It looked a nice sort of a house to Polly.

'Who lives here?' she asked. 'Is it the master's house?'

'No!' laughed the man. 'The Greg family have

always lived in the orange house beside the mill but the present master, Mr Robert, had a right grand place built for his family, further away from the mill noise and smoke. No, this house here is for the apprentices. Near on ninety children as things are at present. I'm Mr Dawson, superintendent of the place along with my wife, Mrs Dawson.' He opened the door. 'Come inside now. The doctor will be in our parlour. This way.' He led them through a room with desks and benches and a blackboard on the wall. 'Schoolroom,' he said. 'They eat in here too. Come on.' He led them into a room furnished with curtains and upholstered chairs, and a shiny table behind which sat an elderly man with a big bald forehead and a fluff of white hair down each side of his head. 'Dr Holland,' said Mr Dawson. 'These two lasses here are for you to assess as possible apprentices. I'll leave you to it.' He bowed slightly, and out he went.

Dr Holland looked at Polly and Min, his gaze settling on Min.

'How old are you?'

'They said ten at the workhouse, sir,' said Min.

'You're small for ten.'

'She's really strong, though,' said Polly. 'She can lift me up.' Polly caught Min's eye and gave a little nod, and Min took the hint and clasped her arms around Polly's middle and lifted as Polly pushed herself on to tiptoe, tipping from side to side and laughing as if it was Min holding her in the air and making her wobble. Dr Holland couldn't see their feet because he had the table in front of him. 'Put me down, Min!' said Polly, dropping her heels and crouching slightly to make it look as if Min had done just that.

'Very good,' smiled the doctor. But the exertion of trying to lift Polly had made Min cough, and the doctor's frown came back. 'Let me listen to your chest, please.' He got up and limped over to them. 'Do you cough much?'

'No, she doesn't,' said Polly before Min could answer. 'Only with the dust from the roads these last few days.'

There were sudden shouts from the other side of the door. It burst open, and into the room came a man holding up a hand that was dripping with blood. Dr Holland immediately lifted the man's bleeding hand up high, and told him to sit down. Polly and Min were hurried away by a woman who'd followed the bleeding man into the room.

'This way,' she said. She was plump and red-cheeked. 'I'm Mrs Dawson. You can come and help me put out the laundry until Dr Holland is free to finish examining you.'

'We'll carry it all,' said Polly, lifting the wicker basket heavy with sodden grey clothing. Out in the sunny garden, Mrs Dawson stood, arms folded, smiling, as the two girls spread the shirts and breeches on the grass and bushes to dry.

'Well, thank you, girls,' she said.

When Dr Holland came out of the house, placing his top hat on his old head, he looked startled to see them. 'Oh, goodness, I'd forgotten about you two,' he said. 'And I'm due to dine with Mrs Greg now.' He took his watch from his pocket.

'You carry on, Dr Holland,' said Mrs Dawson. 'I can tell you from the way they've just helped me that these are good strong girls.'

'In that case,' smiled Dr Holland. 'Tell your husband that they are passed as fit.' And he hurried off.

'There,' said Mrs Dawson taking the empty basket. 'I'll tell Mr Dawson that the doctor has given approval. Then he can tell them down at the mill to do the necessary paperwork to let the St Pancras fellow get going on his long journey back to London.'

'Paper work?' said Polly. 'They said it was cotton work, not paper work, here.'

Mrs Dawson laughed. 'It *is* cotton that's worked here, but if you're to be apprentices, it has to be written down, all legal and proper, and signed by Mr Greg to show you're indentured. The money side of things will need sorting too.'

'How much do we get paid?' said Polly.

'Paid?' Mrs Dawson laughed. 'There's no pay for apprentices, my girl, at least not unless you do overtime. You're given a home and food and an education. What I meant about money was the money the workhouse you've come from will pay the mill to take you on as apprentices, and off their hands.' Polly remembered how the carter had paid the Nottingham mill to take the other children. It was strange to think that those men who didn't even know her and Min were writing things about them and handing over money to tie them to this place. But as she sat down at the long table in the bright kitchen of that Apprentice House, shiny copper pots hanging on the wall, a smell of hot fresh loaves of bread steaming gently on the side, and the sun shining through the window, Polly turned to Min.

'I think this is going to be all right,' she said.

Chapter 8

'Think of me as the Apprentice House mother and Mr Dawson as the father,' said Mrs Dawson. 'Firm but fair, that's how we work. It's the only way with so many of you to get fed and taught and rested, and the house needing to be kept in order. The cook is Mrs Mossop. Her husband is a weaver. They live over in Styal village. Then there's an awful lot of children's names for you to learn and all the other mill workers as you go along. More children than grown-ups, mind.' Min and Polly had already been given bread and dripping and a cup of milk, and now Mrs Dawson was pushing them out into the yard. 'I'm going to cut that long hair of yours, Min. It'd be a liability for getting caught in the machinery, would that.'

Polly's hair was already short enough, so she was sent to wash under the pump as Min sat on a stool and Mrs Dawson set to work with scissors.

When Polly turned back from the pump and saw shorn Min she laughed out loud because she looked so startlingly different.

'Your ears look so big!' said Polly. And Min's nose looked more pointy, her eyes brighter. 'You look like a mouse!'

Min reached up to feel her bony head's fine fluff of hair.

'It'll grow back,' said Mrs Dawson. 'And you'll grow in your body too here, Min, with good food inside you. You'll start at the mill tomorrow. But for now you can both help Mrs Mossop in the kitchen.'

So Polly and Min were set to work scrubbing potatoes.

'Can you smell that?' whispered Min, and they both breathed in the promisingly meaty smell coming from a steaming vat in a corner. Polly's stomach ached with longing. Not roast beef, but still something good.

Soon after they heard the bell clang down at the mill

to mark the end of the day's work, Polly heard a rumble of more than a hundred clogs on cobbles, and lively chatter. She exchanged looks with Min, then went to the door to look into the yard. A crowd of children were pushing to get to the water pump outside, to wash. The mill children seemed intimidatingly big, some of them almost grown-up. It looked as if they'd all just come through some kind of summer snowstorm, because they were sprinkled with flecks of white like willow seed. That must be cotton, realised Polly. They all smelled strongly too of oil. They looked so tired it made Polly's stomach tighten with apprehension. Those children had just come out of a world that she didn't yet know, but very soon would.

The apprentices glanced at Polly and Min as they came inside and sat to eat. There were more girls than boys filling the benches. Mrs Dawson gestured at Polly and Min to sit too.

'That's Lily's place, that is. You can't sit there,' said a tall pale girl as Polly and Min tried to sit.

'Oh, leave them be, Nell,' said another. 'They're new.'

'I didn't know it was Lily's,' said Min.

'Well, you do now,' said Nell. 'So shift yourself. Where are you from anyway? You talk funny and you look funny.'

'London,' said Polly. She thought that *they* all talked funny, with a sort of up and down lilting way of saying things.

'Your dresses are different,' said a beautiful big girl with ginger hair and a bosom. That was true. Min's and Polly's dresses were the workhouse-uniform brown whilst the mill girls were in shades of blue and grey. The big girl pointed at Min. 'Do they all wear turd-coloured dresses in London?'

Min seemed to be shrinking smaller as they looked at her. So Polly leaned over the table.

''Course not,' she said. 'King William lived in London, and I don't suppose he ever wore a dress of turd colour or any other colour.' The children nearby laughed at that. The big girl scowled.

The stew did have meat in it as well as vegetables, and it was very good. Polly wiped bread around her bowl to soak up the last of its tasty gravy. They didn't call it stew here. They called it 'scouse'. There were other words that

Polly didn't understand. *At least I've got Min who talks the same way I do*, she thought.

The girls all slept in a big upstairs room full of box beds, most of them shared by pairs of girls. Luckily none of the apprentices wanted to share with a Londoner.

'They're sure to be scabby. Besides, they'll steal your health while you sleep,' said the big girl who they now knew was called Big Ann. 'That's what me mam said foreigners do to you.' There was a murmur of agreement from the others.

'You share with me here then, Big Ann. And those two can have your bed,' said a girl called Dora.

So Polly and Min snuggled together as they had done in the workhouse, penned in by the low wooden walls of their bed, with a scratchy brown blanket over them like a pie crust. Polly could sense the listening ears in the beds all around them. Soon Min was snoring gently, but she lay awake, looking over to a big, arched window through which the moon shone bright. This was a strange place. But a full belly and a bed shared with a friend gave Polly a feeling of contentment that mixed with little fearful jags of excitement when she thought of going into the great, noisy mill building in the morning.

Goodnight, Aunt. Can you feel me thinking of you?

The morning seemed to arrive the moment she closed her eyes to sleep.

Clang, clang. 'Up you get. Hurry up.'

Polly and Min climbed out from the warm huddle of bed, on to cold floorboards. They fumbled into their dresses and pinafores and straightened their caps. Other girls were hurrying past them and down the ladder. Polly and Min followed, and then outside to gasp as they splashed cold water from the pump up on to their faces.

'You two new 'uns are to come along with me,' said Dora. 'I've to take you early so that you can see how the job works before they start up the machines.'

So Polly and Min hurried to follow Dora down the cobbled lane to the huge mill buildings. Those buildings were quiet now. Dora told them to leave their clogs outside the mill door. 'You've to have bare feet inside the mill,' said Dora. 'The iron shodding on the clogs can spark a fire if you kick one of the machine frames.

Besides, clogs're too slippery on the floor, and you'd be sure to skid into a machine. D'you know which floor you're to be working on?' Polly and Min shook their heads.

Inside, a great hulk of mill building stank damply of oil and old sweat. Dora took Polly and Min into a vast room crammed full of rows and rows of metal frames rigged with thousands of rows of cotton threads, frozen still and waiting for the working day to begin. 'Here are the new ones for you, Mr Rudge. I don't know if they're for spinning or not?' Mr Rudge was the man in the frock coat they'd seen the day before. He looked Polly and Min up and down.

'You're small,' he said. 'Are you quick?'

'Yes,' said Polly, just as a tall, black-haired man in another fine outfit came into the room.

'Oh, Mr Greg.' Mr Rudge straightened his shoulders and looked up at the master. 'These are the two new apprentice girls, sir. I'm thinking of setting them to scavenging.'

'Excellent,' said Mr Greg with hardly a glance at the girls before he turned fully towards Mr Rudge. 'I want production improved, Mr Rudge. We were down on our cloth production last month and it won't do. Do you understand?'

Mr Rudge nodded, going pink. 'Certainly, Mr Greg.'

Off strode the master to see to other things. Polly saw the obsequious smile slip from Mr Rudge's face the moment Mr Greg turned from him.

'Right, then.' Mr Rudge handed Polly and Min a small leather pouch each. 'Listen well to what I'm telling you because your very lives might depend upon it.' He wagged a finger and looked each of them in the eye to make sure they were paying attention. 'Your job is to collect the cotton waste that we call "flue" from the floor and the machines. If that flue isn't picked up it'll clog the machine parts, jamming and slowing the workings, and that's one good way to reduce production. You've just heard the master. Production must improve.'

Mr Rudge made the girls roll up their sleeves and tuck their cap strings under their cotton caps.

'Anything loose will get caught in the machines, and that includes fingers and hair. You've to be quick and keep your mind on the job.'

That job was to scuttle about the floor each time the row of spinning mules pulled back along runners, before coming forwards again. You couldn't stand up to do the job because the rows and rows of thread lined the air above your head and trapped you under them like fine cage bars. You had to crawl and scuttle and swim on your belly across the floor under the machines.

'These mules don't care whether you're in the way of their travel or not. They'll keep powering back and forth like pistons, over and over, so you've to fit in with that, or . . .' *Smack!* Mr Rudge punched a fist into his other hand. 'That or the spinner has to halt the machine. But that can't be done fast, and every stoppage gets us further behind . . .'

. . . *with production*, thought Polly.

The spinning room had filled with workers now, and an ominous rumble of sound and a very slight quivering of the whole building made Polly guess that the waterwheel had been set in motion. She felt as though she was inside a beast that had woken up. Soon broad leather bands were whirring fast, high up over the lines of machines, wound by the waterwheel and cogs. Mr Rudge looked around, then held up a hand and bellowed, 'Be ready, all!' His shout made Polly jump, and Min cover her ears. 'Engage!'

Spinner women and men reached to attach their mule's mechanism to cogs being spun by those bands. The whole building seemed to shudder as the machines started up, a great cacophony of clatter and rumble filling the air and juddering the floor under their bare feet. Metal spider arms grabbed and slammed, and wheels trundled over rails, as the workers' own arms reached, pulling and threading in rhythm with the machines.

'Johnny!' bellowed Mr Rudge over the noise, and he beckoned to a small boy in breeches and no shirt. *It must be easier crawling in breeches than a dress*, thought Polly. There wasn't much flue under the machines yet because they had only just started up, but Mr Rudge made the boy get under the threads as the machinery drew back, pretend to pick bits and put them in a pouch, then scuttle out backwards quickly as the spinner pulled the frame rumbling back over the rails.

Mr Rudge then pointed at Min to take a turn under the machine. Nobody bothered much even trying to talk now that the machines were going. Communication seemed to be done with gestures, pointing and making faces. Polly gave Min a quick smile to encourage her. Then she crouched down to watch nervously as Min waited for the moment when the machinery, pulled back.

Min crawled fast under its threads, turning and scuttling back quickly before the machinery began rolling back on its return journey. Min hadn't picked up any flue, but even so she got tangled in her dress coming back out that first time. Polly reached under and yanked Min out before the machinery got her. Mr Rudge seemed to think that was funny, his face wobbling with laughter even though they couldn't hear it. Then he walked away into a blizzard of cotton fluff that was in the air everywhere now, waving a hand to indicate that they should get on with the job.

Polly and Min twisted their dresses and knotted them to one side. It looked silly, but they saw that's what the other girl scavengers did.

Polly was soon closely acquainted with the oil-soaked planking floor up and down that line of screeching back and forth mules. Under rows of twisting, quivering stretched lines of white thread she breathed a mixture of oil fumes and cotton fluff, which choked and sickened and made her cough. It was worse if you gasped a breath after the cough, sucking in a mouthful of the tickly fibres. She quickly learned to keep her mouth clamped shut, breathing just through her nose.

Polly's head soon throbbed with the sounds and smells and concentration and fear that went on and on. Picking, picking at small balls of fluff that fell and settled like snow, she stuffed her flue bag as fast as she could because the only moment to sit up from a stooped crouch was when you emptied the flue bag into a bigger bag at the side of the room.

Breakfast break happened partway through the morning when the apprentice children all went outside into welcome clear air. There they were given a ladleful of thick grey porridge slapped into a hand to eat and lick from grubby fingers in the sunshine. A big lad deliberately shoved Polly to make her drop part of her porridge dollop on the ground, then giggled in a honk because his voice was breaking, and the other children laughed at that more than at Polly. Min shared her porridge with Polly. But the girl serving gave them each more anyway. It seemed you could have as much as you wanted.

Then it was back to the same work. The sound of many thousands of wheels and spindles whirling and screeching vibrated the building as the machines tugged and twisted miles and miles of cotton into thread. The air in the mill grew hotter and damper and thicker with cotton fibres as the day wore on, the windows kept shut to keep the fug inside. At noon the bell rang for the midday meal, and the apprentice children all clomped up the cobbled lane back to the Apprentice House to sit at tables and eat cold porridge left over from breakfast, but with a sweet baked onion each too. Meanwhile, children from Styal village ran up the path to eat with their parents at home. Polly thought longingly of sharing meals with Aunt in their cellar room. She asked Min, 'Do you like this better than the workhouse?'

Min gave Polly a pale-faced small smile. 'I like it when we go outside,' she said. Polly had noticed that Min still looked around at the trees and the river as if they were wonders, and Polly supposed that actually they were. Min had seen her first swan on the millpond, and been amazed at its size and beauty. 'I never . . . well, I never ever . . .' She hadn't been able to put it into words.

'Hey, London girl!' said the boy with the honky voice, pointing at Min now. 'Say "girl". Go on!' The boy was from Liverpool, as most of the apprentice children were, so they all pronounced 'girl' as 'gairl', and they thought it was hilarious when Min said it as 'gel'. They turned to Polly. 'Go on, you say it now.'

'Gairl,' said Polly, copying their own accent, and making it sound silly. They didn't think that was funny. Big Ann turned on Polly.

'You think you're so special, just because you've come from London where the queen lives. Well, you're not!'

Any answer to that would be the wrong answer, so Polly kept her mouth shut.

Then it was inside again, and back to trying to concentrate on picking up the flue, all whilst working nimbly enough to dodge moving machinery. Polly tangled her legs in her dress more than once, having to go on to her belly and swim herself across the oily floorboards to escape the mule in time. Her sore fingers filled bag after bag of flue picked from the floor and machine frames.

The place smelled of sweat as well as oil as the air got hotter and damper once more. Polly went to the water bucket and drank from the dipper ladle often, trying to swallow down the fluff that got into her mouth through her nose, as well as to water her parched insides. She sometimes saw Min's small figure through the thick white air. She could see her friend coughing even though she couldn't hear the coughs amidst the mechanical din.

For that first week every day was much the same. Long hours of work, then the short sharp walk up to the Apprentice House for meals and maybe a lesson in the big room. The boys worked at writing and sums. The girls learned letters and numbers too, but mostly did sewing, which Polly loved. She and Min were set hemming handkerchiefs for the master's household. That was something Polly could do fast and well, her fingers working tiny, invisible stitches on the folded cotton of a far finer quality than the rough calico spun and woven in the mill.

'That's very nicely done,' said Mrs Dawson, checking Polly's work. 'Oh, but Min, those stitches of yours are far too big.'

It was thanks to Aunt and lots of practice that Polly had such good stitching skills. '*Get the trick of doing it fine, and the better jobs will come your way,*' she'd told Polly often enough. '*And always be a little bit clever to help yourself whilst you're at it.*' Now Polly turned her pinafore-apron skirt inside out on her lap, and quickly attached one of those white handkerchief squares to it, stitching down two sides and along the bottom, but leaving the top open.

'What are you doing?' asked Min.

'Pocket,' whispered Polly, glancing around to make sure none of the other girls had noticed. 'To keep things in.' She was thinking of her St Pancras shilling and Aunt's red rose, which were both in an old flue bag tied under their bed at the moment. A pocket would let her gather odd scraps of thread or fabric that might be useful for something. '*You never know what you might need, or when, so peck it all up.*'

'I was sure there were a full dozen handkerchiefs

here, girls, and now I can count only eleven,' said Mrs Dawson, frowning at the white pile.

'Shall I count them for you?' said Polly sweetly. She did count, finding, 'There's twelve, Mrs Dawson.'

'Oh, how silly of me,' said Mrs Dawson, putting the pile aside, satisfied.

On Sundays the children dressed in clean clothes and walked in pairs the two miles to Wilmslow for the morning church service. Min wore her blue ribbon on Sundays, tied in a bow around her neck since her hair was too short to tie anything into. They talked as they walked along the track and into the village.

'Look at that,' said Min, pointing to a cottage window that had blue curtains either side of a bright red geranium planted in a bowl on the sill. The workhouse didn't have curtains or flowers on sills, and neither did the Apprentice House except in the supervisors' parlour. 'Let's have curtains like that when we get a house,' said Min. Polly liked the fact that Min talked of 'when' and not 'if'.

'We'll have plates with patterns on too,' said Polly. 'Maybe a dresser for them to sit on so we can look at them when we're not eating off them.' Aunt had one plate that had a picture in blue on it of a tree and a bridge. Mrs Proudfoot must have that plate now.

Polly walked quietly for a bit. She'd learned from Big Ann that you had to work as an apprentice, living in the Apprentice House, until you were eighteen. Could Aunt wait eight years in that lunatic ward until Polly came for her? She would have to run away before then. But how could she get all the way back to London with just one shilling? And what about Min? Besides, there were things here at Quarry Bank that she liked. She was even beginning to get on with some of the other apprentice children. She could make them laugh if she imitated Mrs Dawson or Mr Rudge. And walking in the sunshine, talking to Min, was always nice, especially knowing there'd be a good meal when they got back from church. She and Min had pulled carrots from the garden that morning, and the thought of their sweetness made her mouth water.

'We'll have a garden and grow things when we get our house,' said Polly.

'Can we grow flowers too?' said Min. 'Bright colours?

And maybe medicine things like the ones that Dr Holland uses?' Dr Holland had prescribed plant teas and also antimone drops in a little wine to help with Min's cough.

'Some of those medicine plants you can just find on waysides and the like, without growing them,' said Polly. 'So long as you know when and where to look. Aunt and I pick nettles for soup or tea when they're spring fresh. That's good for your blood, she says. And we walk out to get hips and acorns from the hedges and woods in the autumn. Then rosehip syrup stops you getting ill when the winter cold comes.'

'I wish I knew how to do cures,' said Min. 'We could get our own antimonal stuff so I never cough again.'

'I don't know if antimonal is even made from plants,' said Polly. 'But Aunt would know; if only we could ask her. She learned all those things from the lady she used to work for.'

When, at lunchtime, Mrs Dawson asked who could go and collect some comfrey for a poultice that Dr Holland had prescribed for a child's swollen leg, Polly's hand shot up.

'I know what comfrey looks like,' she said. 'Hairy leaves. White or pink flowers. I'll need Min to hold the basket while I pick the leaves, though.'

So the two of them were allowed to go beyond the Apprentice House garden and into fields and woods above the mill, free for a while that Sunday afternoon.

They found and picked comfrey that was growing at the base of a stone wall, and they filled the basket with its leaves. But they didn't hurry back. Min loved to be told what plants and animals were, and that made Polly see things anew.

'See that?' she said, pointing to a beech tree with a blackened hole in its trunk. 'That must've been hit by lightning.'

'Let's look inside it,' said Min.

Min was so small she could climb right inside the hole . . . then came back out with a tearing noise as her pinafore caught on a twig. 'Oh, froggits, look at me pinny! What'll I tell Mrs Dawson?'

'Never mind that,' said Polly. 'We're doing her a favour, remember. But we could use this tree hole to keep things in. I'll put my workhouse shilling in there.

And Aunt's rose. I reckon things'll stay safer there than in the house. We can save things together, safe and secret in that tree.'

They made sure to remember the look of the tree from all sides, and to remember that it was five big strides off the main track through the wood.

'Going west from the path,' said Polly, squinting a bit. 'Look, the sun's going down that way so that's west. Lummy, Min. If the sun's going down we'd best get back quick or we'll be for it.'

They were still planning their house as they lay in bed that night.

'I like the colours that lady at the front of the church was wearing today,' said Min. 'I want flowers in our garden those colours. Dark and light reds.'

'What are you two talking about?' said Betsy from the next bed.

'Just that lady in church's dress with the flowers on,' said Polly, and there were murmurs from the other girls who had also noticed its beauty and impracticality. 'Her skirt was just about big enough to live under!'

'I'd like to see her try feeding the carding machine

wearing that!' said somebody.

But when the others had gone quiet, Polly whispered to Min, 'You'll soon have flowers on your dress, Min, too. I promise.'

'How?'

'Wait and see,' said Polly.

Chapter 9

'Oh, I've dropped me needle,' said Polly the next time they did sewing in the schoolroom after work.

'Well, that was clumsy of you, wasn't it,' said Mrs Dawson, busily winding wool.

'I'll find it, no bother,' said Polly, going down on hands and knees, seeming to search but actually pinning the needle into the hem of her dress. Polly fussed around on the floor some more. 'Oh dear, I can't see it anywhere.'

'Then it must've fallen into a gap between floor boards,' said Mrs Dawson.

'I'm ever so sorry,' said Polly. And that was that.

She took a sharp little knife from Walter, the boy who'd pushed her and laughed at Min when they first arrived. He used that knife for whittling sticks and shaping quills and cutting string. Stealing the knife was mean, Polly knew, but it served him right.

'*Not all justice is sorted by law, Polly,*' Aunt would say. '*Sometimes we sort it ourselves and save judges and lawyers the bother.*' Polly wrapped the little knife in a scrap of rough cotton, and slipped it into her hidden pocket.

Remembering how she and Aunt had coloured dull plain cotton thread when there wasn't the fine work that offered the chance for taking coloured threads from clothes, Polly got very helpful in the Apprentice House kitchen.

'I can watch those onions cooking so I can catch them when they're done, if you like,' she told Mrs Mossop. 'Shall I drain that spinach for you?'

She had snaffled little lengths of waste thread from the spinning machines, pocketing the threads. Now she put those small windings of threads into the boiling spinach water to be turned green. She did the same in beetroot water to make red thread, and got orange thread when onions were boiled in their skins. The colours didn't come as bright as bought coloured embroidery threads, but they would still sing out against the drab pale brown of Min's dress.

Polly stitched flowers on to Min's dress one night when there was a full moon. She'd kept herself awake as the others fell asleep. Then she carefully climbed over the wooden rim of the bed, and took Min's dress from the peg. She tiptoed to sit cross-legged like a tailor on the floorboards beside the big window full of moonshine. Using the little knife to cut the coloured threads, she pushed a green one through the needle she'd 'lost', and began working it into the underside of that course dress cloth. She stitched and knotted and shaped. And as she stitched she sang very quietly.

'*Olele, olele moliba makasi.*'

She could almost feel Aunt watching, smiling as she worked. Polly had no notion how long it took for the small posy of flowers to form; red and orange flowers with green stems and leaves. She wished she had some blue thread to add a blue bow tying the flowers together. Blue was Min's favourite colour.

The chill of the night and her own tiredness seemed

to disappear as Polly worked. It was odd how doing work you loved could make you feel less tired. The boys might be learning more about how to read and write, but stitching pictures was a sort of writing too, thought Polly. It made ideas into something that others could see and share. And her stitched bright flowers would never wilt.

Next morning when the bell woke them, Polly was tired, but also excited as she watched Min pull on her brown dress.

'What?' said Min, seeing her face.

'When nobody's looking, take a look under your skirt just there,' said Polly, pointing. Min dropped her cap on the floor, then bent down to pick it up and took a peek under her dress hem as she did so. A happy little laugh burst from her, turning into a cough. When Min stood up she had a hand over her mouth, but her eyes shone.

'What's up with her?' asked Nell.

'Nothing,' said Polly and Min together.

Production was down again, and Mr Greg was nagging

Mr Rudge about it. That made Mr Rudge angry, and he took out that anger on the new girls from London.

'You two, work faster. They might not know about hard work in London, but we do up here. That flue's clogging and slowing the machines. Get on with it!'

They did their best, trickling with sweat and breathing that air thick with cotton that made Min's cough worse in spite of the medicines. *The flue is clogging Min just as it clogs the machines*, thought Polly.

'Are you all right, Min?' she asked at the morning break for porridge.

'Yes,' said Min. Cough, cough. She gave Polly a rueful smile. 'Don't you fret about me. Just think about our house. That's what I do. Then I don't mind the work so much.'

But one morning, soon after the machines were started up, Polly crawled out from under a mule and found herself being pulled roughly upright by Mr Rudge. He took the flue bag from her, and pushed her towards the door. *What have I done?* thought Polly.

But this time she hadn't done anything wrong.

'Tom's crushed his hand in the carder. We can't do

with blood marking the cotton, so you're to do his job until he's got bandaged.'

'But I don't know how! And who's going to scavenge my machines?' said Polly. She'd seen the carding machine that chomped and chewed with huge metal teeth in a dark, noisy, smelly room that was even hotter than the spinning floor was. It scared her.

'The other London one will just have to work faster 'til Tom gets back. Keeping those cans coming is the priority. If the mules aren't supplied with cotton, we'll get further behind with production. Get on with it now.' Mr Rudge gave Polly a rough shove into the carding room.

Old Eli, grey-faced and crippled, wheezing in the cotton-thick air, showed Polly what to do. Cotton had to be pulled with big metal hooks from the canvas-wrapped bales stamped 'Liverpool'. That raw cream-coloured cotton was beaten in the scotching machine to shake out dark seeds and bits of stick. It was now softer, and Polly had to ram that cotton from the scotching machine into the carder, pushing it in with a metal rod. The greedy machine's great, noisy metal jaws, their teeth shining with oil, chomped and churned. From another part of the machine spewed a long thin sausage of even softer cotton stuff called rovings, the fibres all going one way. Those rovings poured down into tall tin cans that little lads carried away to the spinning floor. Sweating and swearing and snatching her hands back from the machine, Polly could imagine exactly how Tom's hand had got caught.

Then suddenly Tom was back, his hand fatly bandaged, his face white.

'You're to go to the spinning floor,' he shouted over the machine noise. 'Something's happened,' and the look of fear on his face made Polly feel sick. Throwing down the metal rod, she ran back to the spinning floor.

The spinning machines in the line nearest to the door were still, the leather belt overhead whirling onwards above them. The people beside the machines were as stone-still as the machines, until they saw Polly, and then the looks on their faces terrified her. One spinner glanced down at the floor, and Polly followed her gaze to see red blood.

'Whose?' said Polly, suddenly clammy cold with

panic. Nobody answered. Polly looked all around, and under the machines. 'Where's Min?' she shouted, grabbing the spinner. 'WHERE'S MIN?!' Amid the clatter of the other machines in the room, Polly lip-read the woman saying the words 'accident' and 'been taken'. And a wail came from the depths of Polly's soul as a large hand clamped on to her shoulder and steered her out of the cacophony of the spinning room, out of the building and into the yard.

'An injury,' said Mr Rudge. 'That pale London one, she . . .'

'Min! She's called Min Ogden,' shouted Polly. Then she took a shuddering breath and let Mr Rudge go on.

'The little lass made a mistake, and got hurt for it,' he said. 'She's being cared for. The best we can do now is all of us get back to work so we don't get further behind with production.'

'How hurt is she?' said Polly, so fiercely that Mr Rudge looked her properly in the face at last. He shook his head at Polly, as if to say that she'd be better off not knowing the answer to that question. 'How bad?' She glared at him, waiting. He rubbed a hand over his head.

'They say that she coughed sudden, and that took her head to the drive band and it caught the string from her cap, and that whipped her up and smashed . . . well, it did just as I warned you girls would happen if . . .'

'Where is she?' Polly's hands were clasped together, her voice wailing. 'Please, Mr Rudge, tell me!'

'They cut her free good and quick, and she's being taken in a cart to Manchester Infirmary. We'll no doubt all be praying for her.'

'But where's Dr Holland? He'd know what to do.'

'It's not one of his days.'

'I need to go to Manchester to be with her,' said Polly, lifting her clasped hands, pleading. 'I'll work overtime for free to make up, however long you like later. Just so Min's not on her own, and I can talk to her, and . . .'

'No,' said Mr Rudge.

'But . . .'

'No.'

Mr Rudge pushed Polly, stumbling, back into the mill. 'You've to do the work of two now that she's gone. We can't get further behind with production. Mr Greg . . .'

Polly let out a cry of emotional pain that made Mr Rudge pause. 'The infirmary truly is her best chance, you know.'

Chance of survival is what he meant.

'If you do as you're told and get back to work, then I promise I'll tell you as soon as there's news. When the carter gets back.'

So Polly went back to work, the others all watching her. But she was oblivious to them. Whilst her body did the job automatically, diving under machines, snatching at flue, scurrying back again, Polly's head was full of imagining Min being whipped upwards by her cap strings to be smashed by that great waterwheel's force winding the leather straps that powered the machines. On hands and knees, hands shaking, she picked and dodged the machine parts that slammed back and forth.

Oh, Min, keep strong! she thought. Polly travelled in her mind with Min in the cart, jolting along the roads to the smoke and noise of Manchester. Could Min tell that Polly was thinking of her? *Think about our house, Min. The curtains. The flowers.* Were those thoughts a kind of praying? *God, if you truly are a kind father who can do*

miracles when you want to, make Min better now. She's
the kindest and best and deserves your help more than
most. Then Polly sang to sooth Min, and sooth herself.

'*Olele, olele moliba makasi*

Olele Mboka na ye, mboka, mboka kasai-i.'

The other children saw her mouth moving, making
strange words, and they wondered if she'd gone mad
with grief. They avoided Polly at meal breaks, and that
evening in the Apprentice House their eyes slid over her to
somewhere beyond. Polly's fierce, desperate face repelled
them. Polly didn't mind. The only one she wanted was
Min. There was still no news from Manchester. Mrs
Dawson tried to be kind.

'More mutton, Polly?' She held a slice of pink meat
from a fork over Polly's bowl. 'You can have Min's share
as well as your own if you like, lass.' Polly shoved the
fork away so that the meat fell, slap, on to the floor. She
got up from the bench and ran outside. She heard Mrs
Dawson exclaim, 'Well!'

Then Polly was running, away from the Apprentice
House, away from the mill, up through the village and
on along the road that led towards Manchester . . . where

she saw a cart coming towards her. It was a Quarry Bank cart. She recognised the driver. Polly stood in the road, and shouted, 'Stop, please stop! Where's Min?'

'Whoa,' said the carter, pulling on the reins. Then he looked down at Polly. 'I'm sorry, lass,' he said, shaking his head slightly. And Polly knew then the truth that she couldn't bear. She crumpled down on to the road.

'No,' she sobbed. 'No!' The man jumped down from the cart, bending over her and patting her back as if she was an upset horse.

'I'm that sorry, lass. I can see you must have been fond of her. Sister of yours, was she?' Polly nodded. Min was as good as a sister. Better, even.

Was. How could Min be in the past when only this morning . . .?

'Climb up,' said the man, helping Polly on to the seat. 'I'll get you back to the Apprentice House.'

But Polly ran. She ran into the woods, to the tree with the hole in it. She reached her arms around the solid trunk, inside which hid her and Min's secrets.

'Min!' she shouted.

But there was no reply.

It was a warm August evening as Polly walked slowly back to the Apprentice House, but inside she was a wild, cold blizzard of grief. Mrs Dawson held her as she howled.

Chapter 10

Polly stayed frozen inside even as the days got hotter and the temperature in the thick-aired, oily, noisy mill rose. She did her scavenging job, and a small boy joined her in scuttling under the mules. She didn't want to know him or his name. She just worked. The only person she wanted now was Aunt. But how could she get back to London? The only person who Polly looked full in the face at the mill was Mr Rudge, and she looked at him boldly, with open hatred. *You killed Min*, jabbed Polly's thoughts whenever she saw him. He'd let Min do the job of two, and that was why she was dead. She didn't say it out loud, but the way he flinched when she looked at him showed that the message was still given and received.

He constantly shouted at her to work harder. She didn't.

Polly wanted Mr Rudge to sack her from her apprenticeship. She did her work badly, even jamming cotton fluff into machine parts to slow down production. He didn't sack her, but he did move her from his spinning floor to the floor above that had a different overseer. There she was put to work as a piecer. That was a sort of promotion, but if Mr Rudge thought that Polly would be grateful for that, he was wrong.

As a piecer Polly had to join-up threads when they broke on the spinning mules. She picked up the two broken ends and twisted them together. The job involved a lot of walking, going from frame to frame whenever a shout went out and a hand went up to show that a thread had broken. *Good practice for walking to London*, thought Polly. She'd heard tales of Quarry Bank children running away. Most of them didn't get very far. *But I've learned tricks off Aunt that'll help me get away*, thought Polly. She planned as she worked.

The world around Quarry Bank filled with fruits and vegetables in the garden and from the farm. Working days shortened to nine hours as the river flow decreased in summer drought. There was a chance for free time in the light evenings. But Polly sat in a corner of the schoolroom by herself when the others went whooping out to play. Mrs Dawson sent her to Dr Holland on one of his visiting days. The doctor prescribed a tincture to lift her spirits, but he also told Polly something.

'You know, Polly, your friend Min was suffering from a cough that was all too likely to worsen into a lung disease that would have killed her before long. I should in truth have rejected her for work at the mill.'

'But . . .' began Polly.

'Quite,' said Dr Holland, holding up both hands as if in surrender, and giving Polly a wry smile. 'Quite so. That makes no difference to the fact that nobody in this world should die of injuries such as the ones she suffered. In fairness, Mr Greg has added safety measures where he can to those infernal machines.' He straightened up. 'But Polly, what happened to your friend is now in the past. The question you must consider is how you will face the future. I feel you now have a duty to live it well on behalf of your friend as well as yourself. Don't you agree?'

That was a new idea to Polly. She picked at a loose thread on her sleeve.

'Have you other friends amongst the children here?' asked the doctor.

Polly shook her head. 'I'm different from them. They don't like me.'

'I expect they're interested to hear about London, aren't they?' said Dr Holland. He put a stopper in the tincture bottle, and stood up. 'Spend time in the garden, Polly. Being outdoors can cheer a soul.'

The doctor must have told Mr or Mrs Dawson that Polly needed to get outside because Mrs Dawson set her to work, hoeing a patch of onions.

When, some days later, Dr Holland saw Polly and spoke to her in the garden, she asked him something that had been puzzling her. 'Why don't we grow cotton for the mill in the garden? Or on Mr Greg's farm?'

'Well,' said the doctor, 'for one thing there isn't anything like enough room for the quantities of cotton this mill gets through, even on the farm. For another, the climate here isn't hot enough. The cotton used in this mill is grown in America, worked by slaves, and that makes it very much cheaper to produce than it could be here.'

'Why?'

'Because, well, do you know what a slave is, Polly?'

'People with no freedom?' said Polly.

'Yes, people owned by other people, given no choice but to work for them. They have neither freedom nor pay, except in terms of being housed and fed and clothed.' He shook his head sadly. 'Slavery is an abomination. But it makes production cheap, and . . .' But Polly's thoughts were no longer on cotton. She had a new thought to feed the anger that constantly seethed inside her now.

'But I have no choice but to work either!' said Polly. 'And I'm not paid for the work I do every working day.'

'Oh, but that's very different,' said Dr Holland. 'Slavery was abolished in this country years ago, and I'm glad to say that it's abolished in the whole of the British Empire now too. You, young lady, are a free citizen of your country, in spite of having physical similarities with those who were enslaved in the past.'

'Am I? Free?' A weight seemed to lift from her. Polly stood up straighter. Perhaps she didn't need to run away after all? 'Do you mean I can leave here whenever I want to?'

'Well, er, no, because, you see, you surely signed a legally binding contract between you and Mr Greg, agreeing to be one of his apprentices, and the terms of that are clear. You work for . . .'

'No,' said Polly, rudely interrupting. '*I* didn't sign anything at all.'

'Then somebody must have done so on your behalf,' said Dr Holland, picking up his bag and making a move towards the house. 'Once you're eighteen you will be free of your apprenticeship and then you can go where you like.'

So I will have to run away, she thought.

As Dr Holland turned to go, he looked back over his shoulder, and added, 'Make friends with the other children, Polly. We all need friends.'

And Polly thought that, yes, having a friend or two to help her run away could make the difference between getting caught or not. Aunt used to say, '*A single thread is a delicate thing, Polly. But twist those threads together and they become stronger than you'd believe possible.*'

Polly did believe it possible, having worked threads in the mill and seen how oakum tufts twisted together into ropes strong enough to hold a ship.

I need to twist myself in with the others, she thought.

So, walking down the cobbles to the mill the next morning, Polly skipped a step closer to a group of girls. They gave her sideways glances, then whispered together things that she couldn't hear. But Polly stayed close to them, watching for a chance to join in. They didn't welcome her, too wary of her, and she understood why. It was like that all day. But in the evening Polly sat in the big schoolroom with the last of the day's light coming through the window on to the socks she was darning, and she looked around at the other girls, stitching and chatting, and boys in their dull jackets sitting and writing slow, loopy words on to slates.

'*You don't notice a brown bird sitting amongst brown leaves until that bird sings,*' was something Aunt said. So, as she sat and darned, Polly began to hum very softly. The girls around her went quiet, listening. Polly opened her mouth and sang properly then, singing the whole of her daddy's song.

'Olele, olele moliba makasi

Olele Mboka na ye, mboka, mboka kasai-i

Mboka na ye mboka na ye, mboka, mboka, kasai-i

Olele, olele moliba makasi

Eeo, eeeeo,

Benguela aya

Oya oya, oya oya . . .

Olele, olele moliba makasi.'

Polly kept her eyes on her darning needle that was drawing fine woollen thread through the sock pulled over her fist. She could feel the other children listening. And when she stopped singing she looked up to see watching faces that broke into laughter.

'Sing some more!' said Little Ann.

'What is that song?' said Nell. 'It didn't sound like proper words to me.'

Polly had never thought much about the words. It was just a song of sounds that she'd always known.

'I reckon that's foreign,' said Big Ann. 'You hear that stuff down Liverpool docks. Don't listen! It's the devil's work, getting inside your head.'

'Don't be daft. It's just from my dad,' said Polly. 'And

he was a good man.'

'Did he work the ships?'

'No,' said Polly. 'He was a soldier.' Aunt had told her that. It was his soldier jacket that gave him a red robin chest. Now Polly sang a snatch of 'Boney Was A Warrior' to take their minds away from the other song that somehow suddenly felt too personal for them to talk about.

'Boney was a warrior

Way hey-ah

Boney was a warrior

John Francoise.

'That's French, that "Francoise" name,' Polly told them. 'That really is foreign. My dad was a soldier who fought against the French soldiers and their emperor, Boney Bonapart.'

'So where's your dad now then? Why aren't you with him?' asked Jim, sitting at one of the tables.

'He died,' said Polly. 'At the great Battle of Waterloo that won that war.' Aunt said that Polly's mother had told her that her husband fought in the terrible Battle of Waterloo.

'Oh yeah?' said Big Ann, leaning over to point a finger close to Polly's face. 'You're a liar, Polly! The Battle of Waterloo was back in '15 and now it's 1838, so . . .' she mouthed numbers and counted on her fingers, '. . . that means you must be at least twenty-three years old. And you're *not*!' She turned triumphantly to tell the others. 'Don't you believe a thing that Polly says. They're all liars in London.'

Polly went quiet again. Had Aunt said for sure that her daddy had died in that battle? She felt cross with her. *Why do you always mix truth and lies so?* she thought. *You've made a fool of me.*

That night she lay in the bed that she had to herself now, and she listened to the hissed whisperings and giggles of the girls in the beds around her, wondering if she would ever have a friend again. Then, 'Oi, Polly,' said one of them.

'Yes?'

'Tell us more about your dad.'

Should she? They were quiet, waiting. 'All right then, I will,' said Polly, folding her arms as she lay there. 'My daddy was actually a king.'

Laughter.

'We're not stupid enough to believe that! We do know that not everyone in London is a king or queen, y'know.'

'Go on, Polly, tell us more,' said another voice. Little Ann. She was nice. So Polly did tell more.

'He was born a prince, with a mermaid queen for his ma.' Polly paused a moment, but nobody heckled this time. They liked it now that it was clearly a story. 'That mermaid queen was so beautiful, sitting on rocks in the sea and combing her hair, that a handsome sailor man fell in love with her, and they had a baby prince, my dad.'

'Tell us what the mermaid looked like, Polly.' Little Ann again.

'She had pink cheeks, and long black hair, a tail like a great salmon fish, and she'd sing all day long.'

'What did she sing?'

'*Olele, olele moliba makasi . . .*' began Polly.

'Oh, that one!' said Sally. Then, 'It does sound proper magical and mermaidy,' she said with wonder rather than mockery in her voice now.

'I never knew that mermaids talked a different

language from us,' said Little Ann.

''Course they do!' said Polly. 'They aren't living in England, are they, so why would they speak English?'

The next day, Little Ann moved up the bench to make room for Polly to sit next to her at dinner. And as the girls all lay in their beds that night, Little Ann said, 'If you're lonely in that bed without Min, Polly, I could come in with you.'

Polly tensed. She didn't want anybody knowing she still cried in the night for Min and for Aunt. 'I'm not lonely,' she said.

'You must be. I would be.'

'Well, I'm not. Because Min's still with me here.'

'What d'you mean? Is she a ghost?'

'Yes,' said Polly. 'Do you want a ghost story? One about a ghost and my great-aunt Jemima?'

'Yes, go on!' said Little Ann. There was no fear in her voice.

She knows it's not going to be about a real ghost, realised Polly. Little Ann's a bit like Min, knowing how you can make up things. So Polly began, 'Well, my great-aunt was out looking for food and whatnot one time . . .'

'Did she steal it? From the queen in London?' said Big Ann.

'No. She wasn't stealing,' said Polly. 'But she does happen to be friends with Queen Victoria, what with her being related to me, and my dad being a royal prince and everything.'

'Yeah, yeah,' laughed the girls. 'Go on . . .'

'Well, Aunt was coming home from the queen's palace with her arms full of pinky sweet-smelling soft lovely hothouse peaches and a jug of thick white cream given her by Her Majesty.'

'What's peaches?'

The question brought Min so suddenly and fully to mind, Polly almost chocked. She did a little cough, steadied herself. Luckily, Big Ann answered for her.

'Peaches are like apples, sort of. Now, shush! Go on, Polly.' So she did.

'As Aunt came down the steps to our place, carrying all that lot, what did she see but a wailing, wavering, great white ghost!'

'Never!'

'She did. So *crash!* went the jug of cream, and there was peaches falling all over the place. Aunt screamed louder than I dare do it here for fear of Mrs Dawson coming and beating us all, but you can imagine it sounding something like a baby that's had its finger bitten off.'

'What did that ghost do then?'

'It reached out long white arms and caught the peaches as they fell, *plop, plop, plop,* then, *nom nom,* that ghost ate the peaches with its ghostly gums, sweet juice dripping all down it and on to the floor. Then that ghost, it looked at Aunt. She was still as a rock, as you can imagine, with the fright of seeing the ghost eating her peaches, and the ghost said . . .' Polly left a dramatic pause.

'What?'

'YOU!' Polly punched the word out loud, and the girls squealed. 'Shh!' warned Polly. '. . . and the ghost said, "YOU are a silly old woman to drop that cream. I didn't half fancy some cream with those peaches. Woowooo!"'

'That's not true!' They were all laughing now, and Mrs Dawson was shouting up the ladder that they'd none of them get any dinner tomorrow unless they were quiet this instant.

They did go quiet. Polly closed her eyes and smiled as she remembered the truth behind the story. Polly, smaller then, had been working buttonholes in a big white shirt. In the fading light, she'd stuck the needle into a finger and risen up, wailing in pain, lifting that white shirt up with her just as Aunt came down from the street into their cellar home. Aunt really had shouted and dropped what she had in her hands. But what she'd dropped were some discarded wrinkled greening potatoes from the market midden, not peaches and cream. And it was Aunt who'd shouted, not the ghost. And the words that had come out of Aunt had been swearing. Polly smiled. *Aunt*, she thought. *I do miss you.*

Chapter 11

As they walked to church next day, the girls wanted more stories from Polly. She couldn't think of one just then, so instead she gave them a game.

'Who's this?' she said. She picked up a stick, thwacked her ankles with it, and growled at Tom in Mr Rudge's Manchester accent and voice. 'You, boy!' she roared. Tom jumped with surprise, making the others laugh. 'Use your toes as well as your fingers to twist those broken threads. We're . . .' and the other children joined in with, '. . . getting behind with production!'

'Do another one!' said Little Ann, hopping up and down beside Polly. So Polly acted out Mrs Mossop screeching as her pan of milk boiled over, flapping her arms, and made them all laugh.

'You do one now,' she told Little Ann. Little Ann did a take-off of Big Ann which made Big Ann cross, and Polly laughed with the others at that. It felt nice.

But on the way home from church, Sally and Lil walked together and bent to whisper into each other's ears. They looked towards Polly with knowing smiles, and she felt a prickle of apprehension.

'Ask her,' she heard Lil say to Sally.

'Poll-y?' said Sally in a wheedling kind of voice. All the children were listening.

'What?' said Polly.

'Sally says that Betsy says that you said to her dad that you were Min's sister.'

Betsy's dad was the cart driver. Her family lived in the village and went to the chapel there on Sundays. So Betsy herself wasn't with them now. They'd all been talking about her some time before today. Suddenly what had felt like friendship with those girls didn't feel like friendship any more to Polly.

'So what?' she said, walking faster.

'Well, Betsy says how can you be Min's sister?' said

Sally. 'Min didn't look like you. She was a lightie and you're a darkie.'

Polly stopped walking. The others went on without her as she stood there with her mouth open in surprise. Of course she and Min weren't sisters in the 'having the same parents' kind of way. She looked at her hand. It was the golden-brown colour of the oil they dipped rags into for cleaning the machines. Min's had been cotton-pale. But the thought that had stopped Polly now was that Aunt was a 'lightie'. Why was Polly a different colour from her? Only Aunt could answer that. Without thinking much further than feeling a need to get away from the giggling girls and the need to confront Aunt, Polly scurried up the earth bank, off the path and into the woods. *I'm going to ask her.*

Polly ran through the trees, looking for the beech tree with the hole in it. She found it, its branch arms reaching out. Polly dived a hand into its hole, and her fingers soon felt the wrapped bundle of hard coins. She brought it out and unwrapped the rag to see her workhouse shilling along with the pennies earned and saved over the weeks by her and Min. How much would a coach ride to London cost? She could find out if she went to Manchester. Manchester where Min died.

Sunday was a good day to go missing. Nobody at the mill would know she'd gone, and at the Apprentice House they'd probably think she was just sulking about what Lil had said to her. They might not even notice she wasn't there until bedtime. Either way, they wouldn't care. Except perhaps Little Ann. Polly thought of the mermaid she had embroidered inside Little Ann's dress with more of the orange, green and red threads she'd dyed for Min's flowers. She'd done it a few nights ago, not telling Little Ann. She'd enjoyed knowing it was there, wondering when it might be noticed. Now she'd never know.

Polly was in her Sunday-best dress, which had only one small pocket to hold her handkerchief. She put the coins into that pocket, then hesitated with the rose in her hand before dropping it back into the tree. *I haven't got any way to fix it in my hair*, she told herself. But she was also cross with Aunt for not telling her proper truths about herself.

Polly hurried through the trees, away from Quarry

Bank. There was an old woman collecting kindling in the wood. 'Please,' said Polly, 'which way is it to Manchester?' The woman pointed to a gap in a hedge.

'That there's a short cut that'll fetch you up on the Manchester road if you keep going long enough.' She looked sharply at Polly. 'You're not from around here. Are you running away from the mill?'

'I'm visiting my aunt,' said Polly. It was only as she said it that she realised she'd slipped into a Liverpudlian accent.

Polly walked fast over the fields, trying not to think of the good Sunday lunch she was missing. It was strange being alone, strange walking freely and in a quiet place. She heard her own hurrying footsteps, the moo of a cow somewhere out of sight, a song from a bird soaring above her. She walked and ran, ran and walked, skirting wide around homes and farms in the hopes that if anyone from the mill searched for her later there wouldn't be anyone who could tell them which way that dark girl from the mill had gone. Once she got to big, busy Manchester nobody would even notice a stranger, and she'd be safe. *I'm on my way, Aunt,* she thought . . .

then caught her foot in a rut on the path, and fell.

Polly's ankle shrieked with pain when she tried to move. *They'll be looking for me soon*, she realised, seeing the sun low in the sky. *Get up, Polly! Get to a road. Get a ride to Manchester by using that money. Go on!* But she couldn't stand. Polly dragged herself along the ground as if she was under a spinning mule, and she reached for a stick from the hedge. Using it as a crutch, she levered herself up, and could then hobble along. It hurt. She was slow and she was scared now, glancing over her shoulder at every sound. She came to a road, and to the right she could see an inn with smoke rising from its chimney, horses tethered and a small carriage. It was a gentleman's carriage, not a public stagecoach, but it might be going to Manchester. No gentleman or lady would give a lift to a dirty runaway girl, though. '*Look to be a lady, and they'll treat you like a lady. Ladies get given things,*' said Aunt in her head. She was in her Sunday dress and had a shawl, which was better than work clothes. But she threw her clogs aside. *I'll tell them that I've lost my shoes*, she decided.

There were stables to one side of the inn, and a boy

was leading a horse out of one of them. Polly limped with her stick to the inn door. She stood up straighter, took a deep breath, then pushed the door open. A warm fug of air and light and laughter came at her.

'Yes? What d'you want?' asked a woman hurrying past with a tankard in either hand.

'Please, ma'am, I am in need of assistance,' said Polly in the poshest voice she could do. 'I have been attacked and robbed. I was knocked to the ground, and my shoes were taken and my money taken too, so . . .'

'. . . you want free eats, is that it?' said the woman.

'That would be most welcome, to be sure,' said Polly. 'But I also need a ride to my large home in Manchester. I assure you my parents will pay a handsome reward to whoever has assisted me. I can see by your kind face that you're a good Christian woman who would want to help a poor . . .'

'Get out,' said the woman. 'I've no time for beggars. Hop it.' Then the woman laughed at her own joke because Polly was more or less hopping with one good leg and stick.

'Ma.' The boy from the stable had come inside. He

pulled at the woman's arm, making her slop beer from the tankards she was carrying.

'Oi, watch what you're . . .'

'Ma, don't be mean to the poor girl. Sit her down and give her food,' he said. Polly caught the look he gave his mother. *Is he thinking he'll get a big tip from my rich parents?* thought Polly. *Or is he wise to me?* She couldn't run in any case. The boy pulled out a chair. 'Sit down, miss, and Mum will bring you food shortly.'

'Will I?' said the woman, putting the tankards down on a table as the boy pulled her out of the room. Polly was glad to sit. She propped her stick against the wall. Soon the woman was back, bringing a plate of bread and cheese, and a cup of milk. 'Enjoy your dinner, miss,' she said.

'Thank you,' said Polly. 'Could you be so kind as to ask the gentleman with the carriage whether he might be kind enough to give me a lift to Manchester?'

'Certainly, miss.' The woman dipped a little bow.

But as Polly ate the bread and cheese, she watched the gentleman and his manservant eating what looked like roast pheasant on the other side of the room, and the inn woman never approached them. A prickle of doubt crept into Polly's mind. She suddenly felt trapped in the inn room. She reached for the stick, pushing up from the table, and started hobbling towards the door. But the woman was there already, filling the doorway.

'Can I offer you a slice of hot gooseberry pie, miss? And cream?'

'*If a thing seems too good to be true, it usually is,*' warned Aunt in Polly's head.

'Oh, um, I just need to relieve myself first, and then I'll be back,' said Polly, flashing a smile as she pushed past the woman. But the woman had Polly's arm now, and was twisting it up her back so that Polly hopped on tiptoes.

'Oh no, you don't,' said the woman, her tone quite different. 'I'm keeping you here until they come from the mill for you.'

'What mill?' said Polly, but her voice came out very high.

The woman didn't even bother to answer as she dragged Polly to a storeroom, pushed her inside and bolted the door.

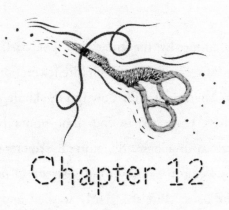

Chapter 12

A cart came from Quarry Bank next morning to collect her. She'd been shut in the windowless dark storeroom all night, so she blinked in the light when they opened the door.

The Quarry Bank cart was driven by Betsy's dad. 'Let me ask you straight,' he said. 'Are you intending to run from me?' Polly shook her head. 'Then you can sit up front,' he said. 'By heck, look at that black sky over there. There's weather on the way.'

Polly didn't speak to him. She supposed he hadn't meant any harm when he told Betsy that Polly had said she was Min's sister, but she still didn't like him for doing it.

It was raining by the time they got back to the Apprentice House. The other children were already at work. Mrs Dawson sat Polly down in the kitchen.

'What have you done to your foot, you silly child? And where's your clogs?' She tutted. 'You're not the first to run away, you know, and near on all of them get brought back.' But she gently washed and bound Polly's sprained ankle. 'Now take off that wet dress. Your Sunday best, all muddied, dear oh dear. But what have we got here?' She took the coins from Polly's pocket.

'That's my money. And Min's. She'd have wanted me to have it,' said Polly.

'Well, it'll be Mr Greg who gets it now, in recompense for the reward money you've cost him by running away,' said Mrs Dawson, pushing the coins over the table away from Polly. 'You've got yourself into a deal of trouble, Polly. Best you can do now is to apologise to the master, saying how sorry you are and how you won't ever do it again.'

Mr Dawson took Polly through the rain to the mill and to Mr Greg's office. Mr Greg sat behind his desk, Mr Dawson sat beside it, and Polly stood in front of them.

'You've to pay back the five-shilling reward Quarry Bank Mill has paid the woman at the inn,' said Mr Greg. 'Taking off the money that Mrs Dawson found in your pocket, that's three and ninepence owing. Then there's the cost of the clogs to add to that, and the loss of your work this morning. Add on the men's time spent looking for you yesterday. Altogether you now owe me twelve shillings.'

'Twelve shillings!' said Polly. 'How can I pay twelve shillings when you don't pay for my daily work?'

'Polly,' warned Mr Dawson with a firm look. Mr Greg held up a hand.

'You will earn the money with overtime.'

'But that's only a penny a go! I'll be working for years before I clear that debt!'

'True,' said Mr Greg. 'You will very likely have to work unpaid for some months after your eighteenth birthday in order to pay it off.'

'That's not fair!' said Polly, fists clenched. When Mr Dawson reached a hand to restrain her, she pulled her arm swinging free, and her fist thwacked on to Mr Dawson's face.

'My word!' Mr Dawson held a hand to his eye.

'Oh, I'm sorry,' said Polly. 'It's just . . .' Her eyes were blurring hot with tears. 'I don't think I'll ever see Aunt again if I have to stay here till I'm eighteen! Wouldn't you just let me go? Please?'

'Insolence!' said Mr Dawson, standing up and quite roughly pushing Polly back out of Mr Greg's office. 'I do apologise, Mr Greg. She will be punished, you can be sure of that.' He half dragged Polly back through the rain, up the hill to the Apprentice House. 'This one's for the attic,' he told his wife.

'Whatever's she done now?' said Mrs Dawson.

'She spoke to Mr Greg in a most insolent manner. And she hit me!'

'Oh my goodness!' said Mrs Dawson. 'Well, some time on your own is what you need, to be sure, Polly. Come along.'

'Please don't shut me up,' said Polly, terrified at the idea of being trapped. 'I'd much rather be beaten!'

'We don't beat girls here, Polly. We never have and we never will. It's not the Gregs' way.'

Up the ladder to the bedroom floor, then up again,

Polly was pushed into the hot, stale-aired attic room, and the door closed on her. She heard the bolt slide across.

Polly folded down on to the floor, knees hugged close. She rocked herself from side to side, and sobbed.

When she finally uncurled herself and looked around, Polly saw that she was in a roof space with sloping walls either side of the ridge down the middle. There was a window in the wall at one end, with rain crying down its glass. The sound of it drummed hollowly on the roof just above her head. On the floor was a night pot and a pile of ragged old clothes. That was all.

Polly hobbled to the window, put the heels of her hands to the frame and pushed upwards. The window did open just the width of a hand, letting in some cooling damp air from outside, but the gap wasn't wide enough for her to climb through, even if she dared to drop from such a height. She tried the door, but its bolt held firm. Polly walked the length of the attic and back, over and over, careful of her still sore ankle but somehow needing to move to calm herself. She was trapped here. Aunt was trapped in the workhouse. Min's body was trapped in a grave. But perhaps at least Min's soul was free? Was she the best off of the three of them? *I will get free and make a life with Aunt*, thought Polly. *I will.* But how?

Much later came the *plod, plod* sound of footsteps coming up the stairs.

'Polly?' The bolt was drawn back and Mrs Dawson came in, awkwardly carrying a jug. 'Bread and water. That's all you'll get today,' she said, bending to put the jug on the floor. 'Why I'm doing this for you as if I was your serving maid, I don't know. It's not right.'

'It isn't,' agreed Polly. 'Mrs Dawson, if I promise to be good now, will you let me out, and then I can do work looking after you instead of you serving me? I won't tell Mr Greg or even Mr Dawson. I could . . .'

Mrs Dawson shook her head, the lace around her cap quivering. 'That's not possible. I'm not the one you have to convince to let you out, Polly. It's Mr Dawson who's got a black eye thanks to you. He says you're to have two days up here, and then you can come out if you're ready to apologise to him and Mr Greg. As for work –' she nodded towards the pile of old clothes in the corner – 'that lot need tearing into rags of a size for oiling and cleaning the machines. Do that, and I might find my way to bringing something besides bread to eat tomorrow.'

'I will,' said Polly. 'But please, can I have a candle for when the dark comes? Or a taper?'

'What, and set light to the whole blessed house? I think not!' said Mrs Dawson, closing the door. *Plod, plod,* her footsteps descended the stairs once more.

Polly drank and ate, trying not to think of the coming darkness. She was used to long dark nights, but they had always been shared with Aunt or others. Never on her own.

Using teeth and then tearing, Polly made a pile of rags and a pile of the leftover seams and other bits that were too lumpy or small to be rags. As she worked, she heard the clatter of clogs and chatter of children returning to the house, hurrying to get out of the rain that kept falling outside. Then sounds from inside the house, deep underneath her. She thought of them all sitting to eat a good meal, then sharing talk in the schoolroom as it grew dark outside. Polly could see less and less in the unlit attic. Then came hollow sounds of feet on floorboards as the children settled into beds beneath her, making her loneliness feel like a solid lump inside her. She was tempted to call out, but she didn't.

Polly shuffled the rag pile to make a sort of nest to lie on. She fell deeply asleep to the soothing sound of rain on the roof just above her . . .

. . . but woke with a scream in the thick, blind blackness of night. Something had run over her face! She could feel the path of light fingers touching across a cheek and into her hair. She sat up, hands to face, heart thumping as she tried to make her brain work out where she was, why, and what was happening.

'Who's there?' she asked in a shaky voice. Was it really a ghost? It was so completely thick-black that Polly couldn't see anything except the blackness that seemed to be pressing in on her, making her barely able to breathe. She wiped her hand over and over where those fingers had touched her, yet she could still feel their touch distinctly. Polly heard herself moan out loud. Then she brought Aunt to mind.

'*Ghosts don't bother the likes of you and me, Poll. Except when we decide to invent them for our own purposes.*' Polly laughed a bit hysterically as she suddenly realised what the truth must be. *A mouse*, the sensible bit of her brain told her.

'Go away,' she said, banging the floor to scare it in turn. *A little mouse couldn't hurt you, Polly. Breathe*, she told herself. *The sun will come up again. It always does.*

Polly sat up the rest of the night, her back against one of the wooden struts, her hands holding her skirts over her feet as she hummed her daddy's song and waited for the light to come back. She'd met many mice in her life, but she still daren't lie down in the dark and close her eyes again. *What if it came scuttling over me again? What if there are lots of mice? What if there are rats?*

Daylight came slowly, gently, blooming wider Polly's view inside the attic. No mouse.

She heard the bell clang down below, and muffled sounds of movement and talking descending lower, then the children were out, clattering off to the mill through the rain. *I'm in the dry*, thought Polly, and tried to feel pleased that she wasn't with the others. *I'm not going to spend the day piecing.*

It was a long time before Mrs Dawson plodded up

the stairs to bring Polly a bowl of thick porridge. 'I'll bring you work to do shortly,' she said as she left, bolting the door again.

As Polly looked down at the blob of porridge in the bowl, a skitter of movement caught her eye, making her jump. The mouse! It was back, but in daylight now.

'Oh!'

Polly froze. The mouse was so near she could see every detail of it. Its eyes were like tiny black boot buttons. For all that its brown body and tail had frozen still just as Polly's had, the mouse's whiskers flickered and its nose twitched, sensing the porridge. *It's thinking it can run to safety or run for the porridge*, thought Polly, and smiled. She waited, wondering whether to reach for the porridge herself, or watch and see if the mouse would get brave enough to claim it.

Neither of them moved. Then, very slowly, Polly crouched down. The mouse moved its head to look at her, but it didn't run. Polly reached her fingers into the bowl, and slowly took a soggy pinch of the thick grey porridge and wiped it on to the floor, before sitting back on her haunches to watch once more.

Twitch, twitch, then a quick scuttle and grab. The mouse had it. It squatted on its back legs now, as Polly was. It held the porridge lump in two miniature pink hands and nibbled greedily. That reminded Polly she was hungry too. She reached out towards the bowl again . . . but the mouse was gone.

Plod, plod, Mrs Dawson was soon back to fetch the bowl. And she brought Polly a basket of darning to do. There was a shawl with holes in it that needed mending, and there were lots of holey socks. There was a twist of fine brown darning wool, a thick needle and a wooden mushroom on which to stretch the holes so that Polly could stitch and weave in and out to fill them.

Moving to sit on the floor beside the window in order to have the best light on her mending, Polly worked through the day, jumping up to look out of the window when there was a clatter of a horse passing by on the road. When Mr Dawson came, grumbling, to take away her smelly piss pot, the size and colouring of the purple-yellow bruise around his eye shocked her. 'I'm really sorry, Mr Dawson,' she mumbled.

'So you should be,' he said, but he didn't sound too cross.

The mouse came back that evening to share the bread and cheese Polly had been brought. She threw down crumbs to tempt it nearer and nearer until she could see every fine whisker and each tiny finger on the mouse as it nibbled.

'You need a name,' whispered Polly. 'An important one, since you're the only friend I have up here.' She laughed. 'You can be Queen Victoria. Even though you might be a boy for all I know.' She slowly reached out a hand to roof over the little creature. *I'll pick you up, then we can talk face to face.* But as she closed her fingers around it, the mouse bit her, and she dropped it with a shout, shaking her hand to try and shake off the pain. But she was laughing. 'I don't think Queen Victoria would do that! But I don't blame you,' she said. She knew what it was like to be trapped.

Bored now that she'd completed all the mending, Polly turned over the bottom of her dress and stretched a bit of it over the darning mushroom. Then she used the brown wool to embroider a little brown mouse. The sharp little face, plump body, long tail and tiny brown petal ears. She did little arms and hands, but the wool was too thick to show the fineness of the mouse fingers that had run over her face, or its whiskers. *If only I had Aunt's hairbrush to take bristles from.* Polly pulled a black thread from one of the rags, and stitched a tight knot of an eye, then snipped the needle free.

'Now I have caught you in a way, Queen Victoria,' she said. But she was alone.

Mrs Dawson took the mended things away and brought Polly a bowl of water to wash her hands in. 'You need properly clean hands for your next task,' she said. She came back up to the attic with a soft blue dress belonging to one of Mrs Greg's little daughters. The dress had a tear that needed mending. 'I'm trusting you here, Polly,' she said. 'I've seen that you're clever with a needle, so make sure that you do a right good job of this for the mistress, please. Here, I've brought you my own sewing basket of threads and whatnot. Don't you let me down now.'

'I won't.'

Taking the sewing basket into the light, Polly

carefully took things out of it one by one. There was a pincushion plump with sand and shaped like an apple, spiked with pins and needles. There were cotton threads and embroidery silks, glass buttons, horn buttons, shell buttons, brass buttons. There was a little pair of sharp scissors. And there were remnants of ribbons and corners of fabric that must be left over from Mrs Dawson's sewing tasks. Polly handled every item with slow gentle care, but her mind was scrambling, full of ideas of where she would use that button or this thread if only they belonged to her. Polly found thread of very nearly the same blue as the Greg daughter's dress. She threaded a fine needle, then, taking the soft dress fabric in her rough hands, she gently probed the tear as one might explore a wound, folded in the frayed edges, and stitched tiny stitches that caught together single threads to craft an almost invisible mend. She hoped that Aunt would have been proud of her. *Are you still knitting dishcloths?* Polly wondered.

Polly shook out the mended dress. Its blue was just the colour that Min loved. An idea came, whole and perfect, into Polly's mind. Foraging in the sewing basket for coloured threads, and working quickly now for fear that Mrs Dawson would come back before she'd finished, Polly turned to the inside of the blue dress's sash and worked another little brown mouse, but a finer one this time, made with finer threads. This little mouse had a tiny pink nose and pink fingers. It had whiskers and bright silk eyes. This little mouse had a tiny blue ribbon of silk thread in a bow around its neck. This was a very particular little mouse.

Min Mouse, thought Polly. *A Min who can go into the master's house and see things Min never did get to see in real life. And nobody will ever know that she's there.* Polly added spikes of green grass and pink flowers either side of the Min mouse.

Polly heard Mrs Dawson's plod a ladder and a staircase away. By the time Mrs Dawson pulled the bolt on the attic door and opened it, all she saw was a closed sewing basket, and a smiling Polly holding the neatly folded blue dress.

'Good girl,' she said when she inspected the mended tear. 'I'm pleased. Now you've just one more night here before you'll be back down with the others.' Mrs

Dawson patted the little dress on her arm and headed for the door. 'I'll bring more ragging for you,' she said.

She'd left her sewing basket behind.

Polly watched through the window to see a maid from the big house leaving with a bundle that must be that blue dress with the Min mouse hidden inside it, escaping out beyond the mill and into the fine living of the master's grand new house. '*There's power in secrets, just as there's power in money, Birdie,*' Aunt would say. '*But nothing beats the power of love.*'

Aunt, thought Polly with a tug to her heart. *I want you tell me all you know about my parents, and not just swan and robin stories. And I want you with me again, sharing the good and the bad times. Will I ever see you again?*

Later, as Polly tore the old clothes into rags, using Mrs Dawson's sharp embroidery scissors instead of her teeth this time to get through seams, a seed of an idea planted itself in her mind. That seed grew and branched and flowered. Polly took off her dress, and she pulled from the ragging pile a pair of torn breeches, a shirt and a man's cap. She put them all on, noting where repairs and changes were needed. She changed back into her dress, and set to work cutting and stitching and patching the breeches and shirt. Then she pushed those boy clothes through the narrow gap under the window sash so that they dropped to the ground outside.

Chapter 13

Polly was allowed out of the attic when the bell rang early next morning. She hurried with the other apprentice children out into the rain and down the cobbled lane before she remembered the boy clothes she'd pushed out of the window. She stopped amid the stream of children, clutching her tummy. 'Ooh, I need the privy urgent bad!' Then she turned back to the yard.

Polly didn't go to the privy. She went to scoop up the wet breeches, shirt and cap from the bush below the attic window, then ran to throw them behind the garden wall.

Polly got to the mill door to find a boy there, waiting to tell her she must go to Mr Greg's office.

Nervously, she knocked on his door.

'Come!'

Mr Greg, frowning, looked over his desk at Polly. She stood, head bowed, hands clutched in front of her. *Play the part*, she thought.

'I'm that sorry I ran away, Mr Greg,' she said.

'Well, I hope that you've learned your lesson now.'

'I have, sir,' said Polly, thinking, *I've learned to be cleverer about it the next time I run away.*

Then she was back on the spinning floor, ducking under machines to piece broken threads, working fast amid the din of noise that hit her anew after her days of peace in the attic. The rain of the last few days had raised the water level in the river, and there was now plenty of power to work the machines for the long full working day again. There was no schooling or sewing that night. They all went straight to bed after eating.

When the candles had been blown out, Little Ann called across to Polly, 'Tell us about being in the attic, Polly. What was it like?'

'Well,' said Polly, lying on her back and staring into the darkness. 'I met Queen Victoria up there, would you believe? And she was that greedy for porridge.'

'Be quiet,' said somebody. They were all too tired for talk that night, all of them except Polly soon falling asleep.

Polly was exhausted too, but there was something she wanted even more than she wanted sleep. Aunt. She sat up, listening to the steady breathing and odd snores from the beds around her, and thumps and a door closing downstairs that must be the Dawsons turning in for the night. She waited a bit longer, and then she crept out of bed.

The door at the bottom of the ladder to the girls' dormitory was normally locked each night. But Polly had wedged the bolthole in the door frame with flue so that the bolt wouldn't go into it. Now the door pushed open easily. Polly scuttled barefoot through the dark house, and then out into the stormy dark night that slapped her with cold wet rain.

Rain clouds blotted out any moon or starlight. The icy rain came sideways at Polly as she felt her way to where the soggy pile of boy clothes lay behind the wall. Shivering, she stripped off her clinging wet nightgown.

'*We're all born naked and the same,*' said Aunt in her head. '*Even a queen or a bishop.*' This did feel a sort of rebirth for Polly, being reborn as a boy. *Our plan, Min,* she thought.

It was hard to pull the wet clothing over legs and arms, but the big cap roofed over her eyes, keeping some of the rain off her face. Polly pushed her short thick hair under the cap, and kicked her nightgown into the nettles. *Now, run for it, Polly. Run for Aunt!*

This time Polly would have a whole night in which to get ahead of any pursuers. This time she'd head a different way, west along the river to Liverpool. This time she was no longer Polly. She was a boy, and she'd get work on board a boat going from Liverpool to London. Jem, she decided for her name. Jem for Jeremy, but also Jem like Great-Aunt Jem who was a Jemima. Polly smiled at the thought of telling Aunt that when she got to London.

Bare feet freezing on the wet cobbles down to the mill, Polly hurried through the darkness towards the mill stream that came from the river she wanted to follow. Stormy wind whipped the tree branches noisily on the bank beside her, and she clutched arms around herself to try and keep hold of some body warmth. The mill building gave her brief shelter as she hurried past, and now Polly could feel her way along the metal railings towards the bridge. When solid brick gave way to nothingness under her hands she knew she was at the end of the building. She stepped beyond, thinking she could guess and feel her way to it in the dark, but . . .

'Oh!'

Sudden lantern light dazzled the darkness, sparkling off raindrops that seemed to dance in the air. A man's voice swore loudly. Polly knew that voice. Mr Rudge!

'Is somebody there?' he growled, prowling forward with his lantern.

Polly froze, her back tight against the wall, hoping to hide in the darkness of the mill's shadow. But the lantern light swung suddenly upwards as Mr Rudge lifted it, making its light spill over her. Polly bent her head so that what he'd see was the top of a boy's cap.

'Who in hell's name is . . .'

'Good evening to you, sir,' said Polly, mimicking the local accent and trying to make her voice lower than usual. 'I've come looking for mill work. Would you happen to have any going?'

'What, in the middle of the night?' said Mr Rudge. She saw now that he had a heavy-looking long object under one arm. He dropped it on the ground and stood in front of it.

'What is it that you've got there, mister?' said Polly. *Move the subject away from me*, she thought. But she saw Mr Rudge's face tighten, and knew with dread that it had been a mistake to ask that. *He's hiding something. Something stolen*! she thought.

And suddenly she recognised what it was; a roll of cambric cotton fabric. Being taken from the mill in the middle of the night. By Mr Rudge! Polly gasped. She twisted to run just as Mr Rudge swung the lantern close and used his other hand to swipe the cap off her head.

'You!' The word came out like a growl and Mr Rudge's hand shot out to grab Polly's arm to stop her from fleeing.

'Get off me!' she shouted, wriggling desperately to try and get out of that grasp.

'Oh, you're in dire trouble now, London girl! Trouble the like of which you've never seen before!'

'Not as much trouble as you – stealing cloth from Mr Greg!' shouted Polly. 'All that "lost production". That was you stealing, wasn't it! Nothing to do with us not working fast enough! You made Min . . .' Fear and fury gave Polly a sudden new strength. She did what the mouse had done when she'd caught it. She bent and she bit Mr Rudge's hairy hand. And he did what she had done, snatching that hand away to shake the pain out of it.

Then Polly ran for her life, blindly, desperately, into the night.

Chapter 14

Polly ran, out of the lantern's pool of light, stumbling towards the safety and danger of darkness. Behind her, Mr Rudge roared in rage, and suddenly, along with the sounds of his fury and the lashing storm, came sharp notes of barking from the watchman's dog, and shouts from the watchman himself. *He'll have a lantern too*! Polly realised. *And I can't outrun a dog.* She pressed herself against the mill wall, holding her breath as the watchman and his dog pounded nearer. The dog veered towards her, but a rope around its neck yanked it away from her as the watchman made for Mr Rudge instead. Polly saw the two men's lanterns swing closer together. She closed her eyes with that small-child feeling that if you can't see somebody, they won't be able to see you either. She could hear them, though.

'Nothing to concern you here,' shouted Mr Rudge in a tight voice that was trying to sound cheery. 'It's only me. I'm checking that the head-race gates are holding against the rising river. Call your dog off, Harris, and get back inside. There's no point in us both getting wet.' Polly heard the watchman mumble something, and then his light showed him and his dog passing by her, and away. The dog growled in her direction, but was pulled back and soon gone.

Why did Mr Rudge stop the dog from coming for me? Polly wondered, relieved momentarily. Then she realised why, and terror spiked up her spine. Of course! Mr Rudge didn't want anybody knowing that Polly was there because he wanted to silence her before she could tell anybody he was a thief! *Quick!* she told herself. *Go! Now!*

Polly felt her way with numb fingers along the cold hard wall away from Mr Rudge. But his lantern light and footsteps were coming closer, faster than she could fumble her way from him. He'd see her any moment now! But suddenly the brick wall under her fingers gave way to a door. The wheel room! Opening that door, Polly slipped inside, then carefully, quickly, pushed it shut again.

She was in total darkness now, as if she'd stepped inside the mouth of a sleeping monster, trapped. She knew she must get away from the door in case Mr Rudge thought to check in that room. So she stepped forward . . . on to nothing, and fell, crashing knees then shoulder, landing winded on a cold hard floor. She'd fallen down steps. Polly kept her howl of pain inside her, scrambled to her feet, rubbed her bruised knee, and tried to work a picture in her mind of what shape of place she was in. Where could she hide? She knew that the gigantic waterwheel was beside her, resting deep in a gulley of still water. She could feel its great hulking presence, broad and powerful and waiting.

Drip. Drip.

Was there a door out of this place on the other side? She didn't know. Polly felt her way on hands and knees now, careful not to tip over the edge into the pit full of wheel and water. *I can't swim!* she thought, and she almost hugged the ground as she crawled, all the time feeling as if the floor might tip her into the wheel and water. She heard Aunt in her head. '*Always know how you can get out of any place before you go into it.*' Too late for that.

She reached the far wall, and felt up and along it, but there were no steps here to any door, just solid wall. Polly's throat tightened with the certain knowledge that she was trapped. So the only way out of here was the way that she'd come in. Was Mr Rudge still out there? Quivering violently with cold and fear, Polly crouched in the furthest corner from that door, listening intently, hoping, hoping that all the time Mr Rudge was going further and further away.

Drip. Drip. Drip. Water fell hollowly within the iron wheel.

Then came a shock of a sudden spill of yellow light spreading under the doorway, and something thudding against the door. A rattle of the latch. Polly felt sick. But all went quiet again, except for the *drip, drip, drip.* The light under the door was sucked back outside, leaving her in total darkness again. He'd gone. Polly hugged her arms around herself, shivering and waiting. *Please go away, Mr Rudge*, her thoughts willed. *Stop looking for me, and I'll go from your life forever and never tell what you've done. Please, just let me go!*

Drip. Drip. Drip.

Polly stood up, back to the wall. She counted drips, marking time. She lost count. She started again, and again as time passed. *Shall I go to the door now, and burst through it and away?* She'd waited so long he must surely be properly gone by now.

Drip. Drip. Drip-drip. Drip-drip.

Fear clenched Polly's throat as she heard *drip-drip-drip-drip*. The drips were coming faster, and the watery noise beneath the wheel beside her suddenly grew in volume, sloshing loudly so that, with a *creak* then a *screech*, the great wheel began to turn, churning as flowing water pushed and powered it from below. All in total darkness. How could there suddenly be flowing water? Then she knew.

'No,' whimpered Polly. 'Oh no!' Mr Rudge must know exactly where she was. He had opened the sluice gate to set the wheel turning, and now the flooded river was pouring in water, gushing so fast and full that it seethed beside her as she now ran, blind and stumbling, across the floor towards the steps and the door.

But as she reached towards its latch, the door opened, dazzling her with light. There was Mr Rudge, shouting something unhearable against the roar of the water. Polly glanced to her right to see the great, groaning wheel turning, churning, water dribbling shiny-treacle-black from its blades as it went up and over and around. She turned back. Mr Rudge was blocking her way to the door, standing feet apart, face sneering.

'I've got you now, girl!' he said. His face was lit from below by his lantern, ghoulishly shadowed, and his hot, laughing breath came at Polly as he reached out for her. Polly ducked, dodging away from his hand. She stepped back down the steps, and he followed. Then she ran forward, head down into his stomach to wind him. With a *crash!* he dropped the lantern smashing to the floor. Its light flickered, but stayed lit, dancing shadows of the two of them up the walls and wheel.

Roaring swear words, Rudge grabbed at Polly with both his big, strong hands now, and instinctively she shoved back at him with every bit of strength she had. For the briefest moment, she saw terror on his uplit face, before he crashed, falling, into that turning iron wheel. Mr Rudge screamed a shrill wail that cut through the rush of water noise, slicing through Polly like a knife as she watched, unbelieving, as the wheel's cogs grabbed Mr Rudge's coat and lifted him up, taking him into the darkness.

Chapter 15

The huge wheel turned relentlessly. Machinery hadn't cared about Min, and it didn't care about Mr Rudge either. Hoisted like a scarecrow, Mr Rudge was rising up, soon to be smashed over and then down, down into the floodwater that was powering the wheel. *It's only turning because of him*, thought Polly. *He's the one who set it going. Run!* Her mind told her. *Run!*

But she didn't. In those seconds she couldn't move, watching in fascination as Mr Rudge's boots rose up past her face, listening to the ongoing shrill wail of sound that seemed to come from the boy he had once been rather than the big man he now was. His boots in that flickering faint light looked so ordinary that it suddenly hit Polly that Mr Rudge was just a person, as she was, muddling through life. So Polly did what humanity instinctively told her to do. She reached and jumped, leaping to snatch hold of those boots, pulling on them with her whole weight. And thankfully something gave. Mr Rudge crashed down on to Polly and the stone floor beside the lantern.

Polly shoved the heavy man off her as the wheel screeched and groaned beside them. *Now go!* screamed Polly's brain as she got to her feet and snatched up the broken lantern, spilling oil and light. But still something stalled her. If Mr Rudge had grabbed her in that moment, she would have kicked him hard and gone. But he didn't try to grab her, even though he could have. Standing a few paces from him now, Polly lifted the lantern to look at the overseer as he lumbered up on to his feet.

Pale, quivering, panting, Mr Rudge gazed back into Polly's eyes. She saw fear and wonder and gratitude and failure in them. Neither of them said a thing, but both knew that Polly had held the power of life or death over him, and that she had chosen to give him life. She saw that acknowledged in his eyes. She saw that he had felt terror, and now felt gratitude, and she knew with strange certainty that neither of them would ever tell the truth of what had just happened between them.

Polly half lifted a hand as a sort of salute of farewell, and Mr Rudge did the smallest of nods in return. Polly turned her back on him then, trusting completely that he would let her go. Up the steps she hurried, taking the lantern and leaving Mr Rudge in the dark.

Out through the mill door, Polly was free. She dropped the lantern so that she could be invisible. Because there were shouts in the darkness now, and other lanterns on the move towards the mill yard. She recognised the watchman up ahead, and he had other men with him, all rushing to see why the wheel was turning at night, when it should be still. Polly slipped along through the shadows to go the other way, back to the Apprentice House. Why? She was numb with wet and cold and shock, and the thought of that nearby shelter pulled her to it with a promise of comfort.

She crept through the door back into the familiar dry warmth and smell of old food. She climbed up to the dormitory, peeling off the wet breeches and shirt and stuffing them under her bed so that nobody would see them in the morning. Then she pulled on her work dress since her nightgown was in the nettles outside. She got into bed and lay on her back, wide awake, hot tears pouring down her cold cheeks. It did feel a sort of coming home. But, *Oh, Aunt*, she thought. *What now?*

Chapter 16

Next morning Polly shoved the wet breeches and shirt into a corner of the boys' dormitory. *They can puzzle about them when they find them*, she thought.

The rain had stopped, and the cobbles shone wet in the low morning sun. The trees dripped coldly on them as they all trooped down to the mill to begin the working day. Polly felt as if she was acting the part of herself. She chatted and ate and walked, but all the time she felt herself distant from the others and even from herself. Her mind kept flashing back to the events of the night before. It seemed extraordinary that she alone knew the life or death drama she had lived just a few hours before.

But something was different from the usual morning

routine when they got down to the mill. Mr Greg was there outside, looking unusually dishevelled and tired. One of the managers shouted at the mill hands to wait outside rather than go into the mill as they usually would for the start of the working day. So they all stood under the dripping trees, arms crossed, questioning each other about what could be happening.

'Master's got something to say to you all, so shush your noise and listen,' shouted the man.

Polly looked between heads of people in front of her to the group of Mr Greg and his overseers, standing at the mill entrance. She couldn't see Mr Rudge amongst them. Mr Greg climbed up on to the back of a wagon, then stood tall to address his workers. Polly kept to the back of the crowd, a nervous feeling quivering inside her. Had Mr Rudge told on her after all, when she'd been so sure of him? She was ready to run if she had to. 'Shush!' she told the children round her, and she twisted her head, ear forward, to hear what was being said.

'You will all have been aware of the storm last night,' said Mr Greg. 'That storm has brought our River Bollin to flood, bursting through the sluice gates to set the main wheel turning, out of control, in the middle of the night. But, with luck and bravery, Mr Rudge saved our great wheel.' Polly held her breath. 'The poor chap was injured in the process, but Dr Holland has been called to tend to his bruises and make sure there have been no bone breakages.' Mr Greg fiddled with the black bow at his throat. 'And, um, there is one thing more.' Some people in the crowd were exclaiming at what they'd heard, so Polly pushed a bit nearer in order to hear clearly. 'Mr Rudge told me that he was alerted to the flood problem by apprentice girl Polly Brown.'

'You?!' said Little Ann at Polly's side, and Polly suddenly remembered that as far as Quarry Bank and St Pancras Workhouse were concerned she was Polly *Brown* rather than Polly *Freeman*. Everyone was turning to look at her now. 'But you were with us! Weren't you?'

Mr Greg held up a hand for quiet. 'Mr Rudge told me that Polly Brown beat on his door to report that the sluice gate was in danger of giving way. Is Polly Brown here?'

'She's there!' Hands pointed, then pushed Polly forward to stand below the cart so that she was looking up at Mr Greg.

'I'd like a word with you shortly, Polly,' he said. 'Stay behind, if you please.' Then he addressed the crowd again. 'The river is very full, but the engineers are now watching the sluice gates to be sure that all remains safe. Right, to work, everyone except for Miss Brown.'

It was strange to be back in Mr Greg's office, but this time with Mr Greg pulling forward a chair for Polly to sit on.

'You did well last night, Polly. From what Mr Rudge has told me, we are indebted to you for the entire survival of the great wheel. If that wheel or its workings had broken, it would have cost a very great deal indeed in repairs and lost production.' Mr Greg leaned forward on to his desk, clasped his hands together, and looked at her. 'So, Polly, I'm minded to cancel those debts you incurred when you ran away.' He opened the big ledger book. With a flourish he dipped a pen into ink, then put a line through a sum beside Polly's name and signed it. Then he looked up at Polly again. 'I understand from Mr Rudge that you were particularly close to the poor girl who died, and he told me that may in some way explain your attempt to run away. He suggested we should be lenient with you.'

'Min,' said Polly. 'She was called Min.' She found herself crying then, perhaps with relief but also with renewed grief for Min. She saw Mr Greg feeling awkward at that. '*Get them uncomfortable, and they'll do almost anything to be rid of you,*' was something Aunt said. Polly's tears were real, but she might as well use them. She wiped hands over her wet cheeks. 'Please, Mr Greg, could you let me go from the apprenticeship? I'd just leave here and be no trouble to you any more, and—'

The office door opened.

'Oh, I'm so sorry! I did knock, but you can't have heard.' There stood Mrs Greg, elegant and grand. 'Oh!' she said, looking at Polly as she jumped up to bob a courtesy to the master's wife. 'You're Polly Brown, aren't you?'

'She is, my dear,' said Mr Greg. 'Um, Polly's understandably a touch upset by all that's happened, but we have sorted all we need to for the moment, so perhaps you could . . .?'

'But . . . ,' began Polly, but Mrs Greg was reaching

out a hand to beckon Polly out of the office. 'Come along. I've heard more than one tale about you this morning, Polly, and I would love to hear more. I also have something very particular to ask you.'

So Polly followed Mrs Greg in her rustling russet-red skirt out of the office, out of the mill, to the garden of the orange house, where there was a seat overlooking beds of flowers and looking down to the full-flowing river.

'I think this has dried off. Do sit, Polly.' Mrs Greg patted the seat and Polly sat, tucking a bit of pinafore under her bottom to hide an oily patch on the white. The sound of the river and mill rumbled and rushed in the background. 'This used to be our garden, and I've always been fond of the view from this seat,' said Mrs Greg.

Polly thought how strange it was to be sitting in that garden with the master's wife whilst everyone else was inside the mill, working the machines. She still felt outside herself, watching what was happening, as much as living it for real.

'Better?' smiled Mrs Greg.

'Yes, thank you, ma'am,' said Polly.

'I went to have a word with Mrs Dawson this morning, thinking that she would be the person to solve a little mystery for me,' said Mrs Greg.

Mystery? thought Polly, and she clutched the seat. Had they found the soggy clothing in the boys' dormitory? Had Mr Rudge given her away after all?

But Mrs Greg was laughing. 'There's nothing to be scared of, Polly! We were delighted with it! My daughter Sophy found the little mouse hiding on the inside of her dress sash, and now my other daughters want embroidery on their dresses too. I had supposed it to be Mrs Dawson's own handiwork, and I wanted to thank her. But she told me it had been done by a girl called Polly Brown. And my husband had already told me that a child called Polly Brown had saved the mill in last night's storm, so . . .'

'Oh! I'm that sorry! I shouldn't have been sewing what hadn't asked for, ma'am, only . . .'

'Well, don't be sorry,' said Mrs Greg, patting Polly's knee. 'You have revealed a skill that is exceptional. Tell me, Polly, have you done fine-stitching work before?'

'Yes, ma'am,' said Polly. 'My aunt, she's famous all over London as being the best at it, and she taught me. We did sewing together, until, well, until I came here.'

'How interesting,' said Mrs Greg. 'Tell me, what class of person have you and your aunt worked for?' Polly knew she was waiting for grand names. Mr Moser and the man whose dog had bitten his breeches wouldn't impress her. Polly lifted her head up. 'I have done embroidery concerning Queen Victoria, ma'am.'

'Truly?' laughed Mrs Greg, eyebrows raised.

'Cross my heart and hope to die,' said Polly, criss-crossing her heart with a finger as she looked steadily at Mrs Greg, because it *was* true. It was the mouse called Queen Victoria that she'd stitched with darning wool into her own dress.

'Well, that's wonderful,' said Mrs Greg.

Polly headed back into the mill to work, but with an arrangement for Mrs Dawson to bring her to the Gregs' Norcliffe Hall home next morning. *Then we'll both have been inside there, Min! Sort of.*

Back on the spinning floor, Polly knotted her skirt to one side, tucked in her cap strings, and looked for hands going up from spinners to indicate that a thread had broken on one of the mules. She was soon back into the rhythm of the noisy repetitive work, crawling under the machines, reaching and twisting broken threads together. But, like Aunt knitting those dishcloths, Polly's mind was elsewhere. She was wondering where Mr Rudge was now. Wondering what it would be like inside Norcliffe Hall. Thinking how she would tell the girls that night that Queen Victoria had got her work with Mrs Greg. Thinking how Aunt would enjoy the story of all of this, and wondering if she'd ever see her again.

Polly volunteered to do an hour's cleaning and oiling of the machines after that day's shift was done. She hadn't worked a full day, and besides, now that her debt was cancelled, she could begin saving money again.

With the machines stopped and the workers mostly gone, the mill was quiet, the air clearer, and there was no danger of being grabbed or whacked by machinery as Polly took a tin of oil and a rag, and set to work tending a spinning mule's joints and bones. Her hands were soon black with oil, and her face must have been too as she wiped away sweat. She sang to the rhythm of her work.

'*Olele, olele moliba makasi*

Olele Mboka na ye, mboka, mboka masai-i.'

Will Mrs Greg pay for sewing work? she wondered. *If I earn enough, can I buy myself from Mr Greg?* Masters bought and sold slaves, after all. But St Pancras Workhouse had paid Mr Greg to take her on, not the other way around. It was all very confusing, but perhaps money could get her freedom somehow, and then she could go to Aunt without having to hide.

Crawling out from under a mule, Polly was startled to see two sets of men's shoes in front of her. A memory of Mr Rudge's brown boots, dangling as he screamed, made her feel suddenly a bit sick as she crawled out from under the mule and looked up.

There stood Mr Greg and a man she'd never seen before.

'This is the girl I was telling you about, Smethick,' said Mr Greg. 'The girl who saved the mill.'

'Indeed?' said Mr Smethick, smiling at Polly. 'Well, she seems happy in her work, singing along. What is that you were singing, child?'

Polly blushed. 'Something we used to sing at home.'

'She's from London,' said Mr Greg.

'But it's a song I'm sure I've heard before,' said Mr Smethick, stroking his chin. 'Not in London, but in Belgium, would you believe. It was after the Battle of Waterloo that . . .'

'My dad died at Waterl—' began Polly, then she frowned and fell silent, remembering how Big Ann had said he couldn't actually have died there and been her father.

'It was a fellow soldier called John who sang the song,' said Mr Smethick. He smiled at Polly. 'I doubt a youngster like you can imagine the noise and deadly danger of a great battle. And then the contrasting quiet when it all stops.'

'That's like this mill,' said Polly.

'Not exactly!' laughed Mr Smethick. 'You don't have dead and dying men and horses here, I'm glad to say.' Polly thought of Min and looked at the floor that had been red with her blood. But Mr Smethick was going on with his tale. 'John and I were both badly wounded in the battle, left broken and bleeding, lying on the grass, unable to move. And John began to sing a rather wonderful song. Those eerie sounds of men in great pain around us quietened as he sang, I remember. I'm sure it was that song that soothed us. Sing it again, would you?'

'*Olele, olele, moliba makasi,*' sang Polly, shyly now.

'That's it, I'm sure! John sang that on and around until the sun came up and help arrived. I remember feeling strangely content as he sang that strange lullaby in his rich, deep voice. I felt content in spite of knowing that I might well be dying.' He smiled again at Polly. 'I still think the song beautiful. He was a good man, was John Freeman.'

'Well, come on, Smethick. Dinner will be awaiting us up at the Hall.' The two men turned to go, leaving Polly standing there with her hands full of oily rag and her mind dancing with thoughts.

Freeman, she thought. *Freeman, the same as me!*

Casting aside the oily rag, Polly ran down the stairs after the two men. She caught up with them in the courtyard.

'Please! Mr Smethick, did that soldier, John Freeman, wear red, the colour of a robin's breast?'

The men stopped, Mr Greg pulling the watch from

his pocket, but Mr Smethick turned to face Polly. 'To be sure he did. Our regiment, the 73rd, all wore red coats and black trousers.'

'Not skirts?' said Polly, remembering Aunt once saying that her father had worn a skirt.

'Well, really, Polly, this is ridiculous!' said Mr Greg. 'Go and finish your work, or I'll dock that penny of overtime, saviour of the waterwheel or not.'

Mr Smethick chuckled. 'I assure you, young lady, I've never worn a skirt in my life.' Then a thoughtful look came over his face. 'Mind you, John Freeman must have gone on to wear a skirt of sorts when he joined the Black Watch.'

So he didn't die at Waterloo!

'What's a Black Watch?' said Polly, thinking of the watch in Mr Greg's hand now.

'It's another army regiment. The 42nd regiment,' said Mr Smethick. 'A Scottish one that dresses its soldiers in kilts of blue and green, along with red jackets.'

'Oh, please,' said Polly urgently. 'Did John Freeman have a child?'

'Polly, this is most impertinent!' said Mr Greg.

'Smethick, I do apologise . . .' But Mr Smethick seemed happy to keep answering Polly's questions.

'I don't recall him telling of any wife or child, but then it was all a long time ago,' he said.

'Did . . .' began Polly. But the two men were walking away now. Polly had been going to ask if John Freeman had been royalty.

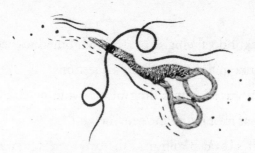

Chapter 17

Back at the Apprentice House, they all wanted to hear from Polly about how she'd rescued the mill.

I didn't, she thought. *I rescued Mr Rudge after I nearly killed him. But I can't tell them that. Well, if they want a mill rescue story, they can have one.* Most of the apprentices were in the schoolroom, and they knew that soon Mr Dawson would come shouting at them all to get upstairs to bed.

'Tell us quick!' said Tom, knowing he'd miss out if the story was told in the girls' dormitory.

'Well,' said Polly. 'Remember how it was such a dark and stormy night? I was lying in bed, listening to the rain and to all the girls snoring, when what should happen but the ghost of Min came into the room. She told me to save the mill. So I did.'

There was silence as they waited for more.

'Is that it?' said Little Ann.

'It's lies,' said Big Ann.

'But Polly did have wet hair in the morning. I remember that,' said Ellen.

'Yes,' said Polly. 'Mr Greg already told you that I went and knocked on Mr Rudge's door. And then it was him who got the help to save the wheel.'

'But was there really a ghost of Min?'

'I felt her there,' said Polly. She hadn't the energy to make up a full story. 'Anyway, because of me helping to save the mill, Mrs Greg is being kind to me and giving me sewing work.' Polly knew that would go down better than her having been chosen for being more skilled at embroidery than any of the other girls.

'Bedtime!' shouted Mr Dawson, coming into the room and clapping his hands.

Next morning, Polly and Mrs Dawson dressed as if it

was a Sunday, even though it was a Thursday. The other children had all trooped down the road to the mill. But Polly and Mrs Dawson walked through the woods to Norcliffe Hall. *I wonder if Mr Rudge is back at work*, thought Polly, glad she didn't have to face him there.

'Gracious,' said Mrs Dawson. 'Look at the size of that house! Well, 'Hall' rather than 'house', I should say, shouldn't I? And what beautiful gardens!'

They went in through the tradespersons' entrance at the back of the Hall. When a maid came to collect Polly from the kitchen, Mrs Dawson surprised Polly with a quick hug.

'Do yourself proud, lass,' she whispered.

Polly was led away into a quiet room with swooping big curtains at the large windows. There were rugs in rich colours on the floor, plump chairs, tables that shone like fresh conkers, tick-tock clocks with finely pointy hands, books on shelves, and flowers in vases. There was a shiny mirror with golden shapes writhing around its frame. In the middle of that mirror Polly saw a dark-skinned girl looking back at her. It took a moment for her to recognise that it was her own reflection, clearer than she'd ever seen herself in Aunt's speckled mirror or in the Apprentice House windows when it went dark outside. This mirror showed someone with big brown eyes in a round face that suddenly grinned.

Chirrup!

In a cage by the window was a small, yellow canary.

'Hello,' said Polly very quietly, poking a finger through the cage bars. It was a pretty cage, but not a big one. Polly could have put her arms around and touched fingers. *A bird can't properly fly inside there*, thought Polly. It reminded her of Aunt shut in the workhouse. Polly pushed the door of the cage open.

'You can fly free now,' she whispered. But the bird stayed on its perch.

A sound of footsteps made Polly jump away from the birdcage. Into the room came Mrs Greg, one of her daughters and a woman carrying some fine bronzey shimmery-brown fabric over one arm, along with the blue dress that Polly had worked on. Polly bobbed a curtesy to them all.

'This, Polly, is my daughter Sophy, whose dress you enlivened with that pretty little mouse,' said Mrs Greg.

'She wanted to meet the clever person who had created it.'

'Hello,' said Sophy. She was perhaps a couple of years younger than Polly, but they both knew that being the master's child made her far superior to an apprentice girl. Polly bobbed another curtsey.

'So, Polly,' said Mrs Gregg. 'I'm hoping that you might turn your needle skills to the *outside* of a new dress of mine so that your work will be on full display this time. Flowers of perhaps oranges and reds against the brown. What do you think?'

'Yes, ma'am,' said Polly.

'Miss Flintock here is our dressmaker, and she will cut and stitch the dress, with you adding embroidery where appropriate.'

So Polly had a strange, lovely day of working with Miss Flintock and fine new dress fabric in an upstairs workroom. Miss Flintock was almost as old as Aunt, sharp-eyed and quiet, but kind.

'Are you interested in dressmaking, Polly, or just in embroidery?'

'Both, really,' said Polly. 'Aunt always wanted me

to be a dressmaker so that I can make a decent living even if I'm like her and never catch myself a husband.' She looked up quickly, suddenly aware that might be taken amiss by Miss Flintock who, from her name, clearly hadn't caught herself a husband either. But the dressmaker was smiling.

'Your aunt sounds a sensible woman with sensible ideas. If you want to learn dressmaking, you can help and watch as I cut the pieces out.'

Cutting pieces from a whole swathe of fabric, using paper shapes to guide the cutting, was something Polly had never seen done before. Mr Moser had always brought the shirt pieces already cut out.

'Here is the front waist panel for you to work on now. Just hem lightly around it to stop the fabric from fraying, then do your embroidery taking into account that a quarter of an inch from each edge will be lost when the pieces are stitched together. Do you want to draw your design before stitching it?'

'I have it in my head,' said Polly. She described her idea, pointing to the skeins of coloured thread, and holding fingers apart to demonstrate scale. Miss Flintock listened and looked carefully, and nodded her head.

'That sounds lovely. Just be sure that it is all as natural-looking as possible. That's what Mrs Greg wants.'

So Polly threaded green silk on to a needle, and began working stems and leaves, adding other shades of green. Then she picked coloured threads to add the flowers. Late in the afternoon she stitched a little ladybird on one leaf. She glanced up at Miss Flintock, and saw that she was watching Polly with an amused smile.

'Aunt always says you should add a surprise so that ladies can point it out and draw attention to their new clothing.'

'Clever,' chuckled Miss Flintock, then she turned back to her own stitching. It was companionable working in the quiet with Miss Flintock, but it made Polly miss Aunt's stories.

As Polly left the Hall to make her way back to the Apprentice House, she peered through the window of the big room where the little canary had been. There it was, still on its perch, even though the door of the cage was open. *Have you forgotten how to fly?* wondered Polly. She wondered that about herself too. She had tried to fly and failed. Would she try again? *Is Aunt wanting to escape her cage or not?* Polly wondered. *And can she answer my questions?*

Polly had asked in the big kitchen at the Hall, and they said that Mr Smethick hadn't stayed beyond yesterday's evening meal. So she'd missed the chance to ask him more about John Freeman who sang to the dying at Waterloo, and who just might be her daddy.

Kicking through the crisp fallen leaves on the woodland floor as she headed back to the Apprentice House, Polly spotted the beech tree with the hole in it. *Oh, Min*, she thought. And then she remembered that there still was a belonging of theirs in that tree. She reached into the hole, felt around, and her fingers touched something stiff and delicate. She pulled out . . .

'Aunt's rose.'

The rose was crumpled, and a couple of the petals had discoloured with dampness, yet it still looked beautiful to Polly. She turned the rose in the evening light, looking at the detail of veins embroidered on each leaf, the curl of each petal, and an idea bloomed inside her. '*Look at things in different ways*,' Aunt used to say, '*and you'll see the same thing anew.*' Polly twisted the thought in her head from *How can I get to Aunt?* to *What if Aunt could come here?*

Next day, back at Norcliffe Hall, Polly showed her aunt's rose to Miss Flintock.

'Where did that come from?' said the dressmaker, turning the rose and looking at its stitching very carefully. 'It's been in the wars and is clearly damaged, but it's been finely made by somebody with great skills. Did you find it somewhere?'

'It's mine,' said Polly.

'Really?' Miss Flintock was clearly surprised that an apprentice child might own something so special. That put hope into Polly's heart.

'Do you think Mrs Greg might want flowers like that on her dress as well as embroidered ones? Or in her hair?' she asked Polly. 'Newly made flowers, I mean.'

'Well . . .' began Miss Flintock. But Polly was eager to say more.

'Because, if she does, I know who can make them. My great-aunt Jemima, who I told you about. She made this rose. She's famous as the best in London at making roses. Other flowers too. I can stitch flowers flat, but I can't make them like this. Not as good as this, anyway.'

'Leave the rose with me for now, and I'll certainly mention it to Mrs Greg when I see her in the morning,' said Miss Flintock. 'Now, concentrate on the job in hand, Polly. You and I have a dress to work on.'

Chapter 18

Polly hurried back to the Hall the next morning.

'Did you ask . . .?'

Miss Flintock nodded. 'I did. Mrs Greg was very taken with the idea of fabric flowers. She thought that her daughters would like to learn the trick of making them too. She asked if your aunt lived locally, and I told her that she lives in London. Is that right?'

'Oh! Yes!' said Polly, surging with hope.

'Give me her address, and Mrs Greg can write to her and ask how best to acquire her services. Tell me what it is, and I'll write it down.' Miss Flintock picked up her silver-stemmed pencil and held it ready over a scrap of paper.

'Oh.' Polly just stood there, not knowing what to say. If she said that her aunt was in the lunatic ward of a workhouse that would certainly be the end of things. Miss Flintock looked up expectantly, so Polly made a play of biting her lip and frowning, as if trying to remember. 'Er, I can't quite think of the street and house number,' she said. 'But I could find the place if I was in London. I know just what it looks like and how to get there. If Mrs Greg would send me to London, then I could find my aunt, no trouble.'

Miss Flintock put her pencil down. 'I don't think that's likely to happen, is it,' she said, and it didn't sound like a question.

As they began to work, the dressmaker had a real question to ask. 'Polly, why are you apprenticed here at the mill when your aunt is so far away?'

'She's only my great-aunt, Miss Flintock. Not that close. My parents died, you see . . .'

'Oh, I'm sorry, my dear,' said Miss Flintock. She was quiet again then, stitching away for quite some time before she said, 'I tell you what, Polly. I will see whether Mrs Greg might possibly have reason to send you to

London so that you can contact your aunt.'

That afternoon, after hours of stitching and with them hardly exchanging a word, Miss Flintock said, 'My own parents died when I was very young.' That was all, and Polly didn't ask for more. But she felt honoured, knowing that the dressmaker perhaps didn't tell such things to many people.

Next morning, Miss Flintock told what had happened when she knocked on the drawing-room door to speak to Mrs Greg and show her the rose. Mr Greg happened to be home just then having tea with his wife. Miss Flintock explained that Polly could only locate her rose-making aunt by doing so in person. 'And,' Miss Flintock told Polly, 'Mrs Greg said, "What a shame because our girls would have so loved to learn to make flowers, but of course we can't possibly send the child to London." And Mr Greg wanted to know what flowers they were talking about, so Mrs Greg showed your rose and explained it all, and Mr Greg simply said, "It so happens that she can go."' Miss Flintock laughed at Polly's astonished face.

'How?' said Polly.

'That's just what Mrs Greg asked. And Mr Greg

explained that in two days' time there will be a cart coming to collect cloth to take to London. He says you can have a lift on the cart, and for the sake of his wife and daughters' need for decorative flowers he was prepared to pay the return stagecoach fare for you and your aunt. If you are truly confident that you can find your way about London to find the right place.' Miss Flintock smiled. 'I think that Mr Greg perhaps still feels indebted to you for the saved waterwheel.'

It felt to Polly as if her heart unfurled wings and soared into flight. She burst out laughing several times as she worked at her embroidery that day, and each time Miss Flintock looked up and met her eyes, she laughed too. It all seemed so unlikely. '*But life IS strange, Polly,*' said Aunt in her head.

'You look like the cat that got the cream!' said Mrs Dawson when Polly got back to the Apprentice House that evening. The children coming in from the mill noticed Polly's grin too.

'I'm to go to London,' she said.

'Oh, don't go!' said Little Ann, surprising Polly with the vehemence with which she said it. Little Ann cupped a hand to one side of her mouth and said to Polly, 'I found it!'

'What?' said Polly, confused.

'The mermaid!'

'Oh!'

'I know it was you who must've done it, Poll. But I'm not showing the others yet.' She looked earnestly at Polly. 'You *will* come back, won't you? I'll miss you.'

'I'm going to fetch my aunt,' said Polly. 'I don't expect I'll be gone more than a few days.'

'The aunt who saw the ghost that ate the peaches?' said Dora. 'Will we meet her?'

'Yes,' said Polly. It was nice to suddenly be the one they wanted to talk to. *Some of them like me*, she realised in happy surprise.

'You could make a run for it when you get to London,' said Tom. 'I would. They'd never catch you there.'

'But I'm bringing my aunt back here to make flowers for Mrs Greg,' said Polly.

Big Ann laughed scornfully. 'You don't, any of you, believe that do you? They'll be sending Polly back to the workhouse, that's what.' The almost-truth of that struck cold inside Polly. Yes, she would have to go back to the workhouse, since that's where Aunt was.

Two mornings later, Polly waited at the Apprentice House for the cart to London to call by and pick her up. She was in her Sunday-best clothes again. Beside her was a basket with some bread and cheese and apples in it, and a letter written by Mr Greg to Aunt's employers, requesting that she be released to come and work at Quarry Bank. Polly also had a purse with money in it to pay for her and Aunt's return journey by stagecoach, but she'd stitched that under her skirt. Polly kept glancing at the window as she sat at the kitchen table, trimming runner beans for Mrs Mossop.

'Mrs Mossop, do you know if Mr Rudge is recovered from his injuries yet?' Polly still hadn't seen him around, yet dreaded meeting him around some corner. Would they both just pretend nothing had happened that night beyond the story he'd told? It was thanks to Mr Rudge, she realised, that she was here, now, waiting to go to Aunt. It was all very confusing.

'Ned Rudge the overseer, do you mean?' said Mrs Mossop, wiping hair from her face with the back of a hand before resuming chopping bacon chunks from a haunch of ham she held in the other hand. 'Oh, he's gone. Returned to live with his mother, I heard. She's not been well, and he's needed there. Why?' Polly shrugged, but smiled with relief. Mrs Mossop smiled back at her.

'Glad to be going back to London, are you?' *Chop, chop.* 'You're a lucky girl. I've never seen an apprentice child given a ride to London before. A ride to the infirmary, or to the graveyard, yes. But a free ride to London, no.' Polly knew she was lucky. But could that luck hold? *Will Aunt still be there?* she wondered. She would know soon enough.

'Anyone there?' came a shout from outside. Mrs Mossop hurried to the door.

'Get going, girl. The cart's here. Don't leave your shawl behind!'

Polly snatched up the basket and her shawl, and hurried to the door. There on the road was a cart led by two horses, nodding their heads and pawing clomping hooves on the cobbles. One of those horses had one brown ear and one white ear. Polly laughed out loud. It was the cart from St Pancras Workhouse that she'd travelled on before! So much good luck! *But perhaps it isn't luck?* she thought. *Perhaps Mr Greg thought to send me back to the part of London he knows I came from?* Thank you, thought Polly fervently. *I just hope Mr Greg hasn't gone and guessed that Aunt is in that very workhouse!*

Polly climbed up to sit beside the familiar carter.

'Well, I'd no idea I'd be giving a lift to you!' said the carter. 'Is the other girl coming home too?'

'No,' said Polly. She took a breath. 'Min died.'

As the cart jerked into motion, rolling along the road away from the mill, Polly told the carter what had happened.

'Dear oh dear,' he said. 'Well, if it's any comfort, and it won't be, I can tell you she'd likely be dead if she'd stayed on in St Pancras Workhouse. There's a lot of death there just now.'

'Is there?' said Polly. 'Why?'

'There's been such an outbreak of putrid fever these last weeks, the graveyard's full to overflowing. I've been glad of the excuse to be away from there and breathe clean air, I can tell you.'

Polly clutched the seat. 'Please, do you know if my aunt is well? Her name is Jemima Brown. She's in the lunatic ward.'

The carter shook his head. 'I don't know that name.'

'*If a thing seems too good to be true, it usually is,*' said Aunt in her head. 'Please,' said Polly. 'How long will it take us to get there?'

Polly draped her woollen shawl over her head, and criss-cross hugged over her front against the autumn chill and the fear of what might be happening to Aunt.

It took three days, but at last the cart was rumbling down King's Road in London, and the large grand frontage of St Pancras Workhouse came into view. There was straw strewn on the road outside. To quieten the noise of wheels and hooves for the sake of those sick inside, Polly realised, and felt fresh fear. She was ready to jump down as soon as the cart stopped.

'Wait up,' said the carter. 'I'm going around the back way into the yard. You can get out there.'

The workhouse walls shaded and chilled the space

where the cart stopped to be unloaded. Polly clambered stiffly down and hurried to the door where a woman with a bunch of keys hanging from her belt stopped her.

'You can't come in,' she said.

'But I've come for my aunt, to take her away,' said Polly. 'I have a letter and money.'

'Then she's a lucky woman, *if* she's well enough to go. Which ward is she in?'

'The lunatic ward.'

'Ooh, they're in a bad way, they are. Are you sure you want to come in?'

The horribly familiar smell of tar as they passed the oakum-picking room was soon overpowered by the stench and sounds of vomit and diarrhoea, which made Polly gag as she stepped into the lunatic ward. The woman hadn't unlocked the door, Polly realised, because there was no need. No one in that ward was in a state to escape their beds, let alone the workhouse. Polly stared about her in horror.

'Can you see your aunt?'

'No,' said Polly.

The women, lying on beds in ones and twos, all

seemed skeletal. Some were moaning, some had their eyes closed, some looked with anguish back into Polly's eyes as she walked from bed to bed. She wasn't sure if she hoped to find that one of them was Aunt or not, for surely all of them were dying? And those that weren't here dying must already be dead and buried. A hand to her mouth, Polly walked and looked, hoping, despairing.

'She's not here,' she said at last, and her voice came out in a sob. 'Does that mean she's dead?'

'You need to go to the office where Mr Scrivens can look and see what's recorded by her name in the book. I'll just call somebody over to show you the way.' Then the woman shouted down the corridor. 'Brown? You're needed.'

And Polly looked up to see tall bony Aunt coming towards her. Both of them froze, staring, not believing for a moment, before they ran, and Aunt's long arms came around Polly to hold her tight.

'My Poll!' said Aunt.

Polly said nothing at all, but sobbed and laughed and hugged very, very hard.

'Well I never,' said the nurse.

Chapter 19

The workhouse didn't want to lose Aunt. She'd proved herself so sane and useful as a helper in caring for their sick that they'd even paid her the odd penny or two. But neither did they want to upset Mr Greg of Quarry Bank Mill who supplied the fabric for their sheet-making. Seeing the power of Mr Greg's letter on Mr Scrivens, Polly promised herself that somehow she would learn to read and write beyond the basics she'd learned in the Apprentice House schoolroom. That letter was just a bit of paper with black squiggles on it, but it had made Mr Scrivens put on his spectacles and stand up, reading with his head doing little bows as if Mr Greg was in the room.

'We will, sir,' he said, when he finished it.

Polly and Aunt held hands tightly as they walked out of the workhouse door.

'Come on, little sparrow. Time to fly!' said Aunt, shaking Polly's hand. Without discussing it, they both instinctively headed towards what had once been their home. As they walked, Polly told Aunt about Quarry Bank Mill, and why Aunt was wanted there now for work. She told her about the mill's machines, its great waterwheel, about Min, about Big Ann and Little Ann and the Dawsons and the Gregs. She didn't tell about Mr Rudge, not yet. But she told about the hills and woods and mill air full of fluff and noise, about the Apprentice House full of so many children, about the grand gracious Hall where she had sewed things for Mrs Greg and her family, where there was a canary in a cage and where Aunt would sew things with Miss Flintock. As Polly talked, they arrived back at their old basement home.

But of course it wasn't theirs now. They stood and stared down the steps to the shut door that suddenly burst open as two boys ran out, up the steps, and away. Through the grubby window they could see movement of other people inside.

'Our stuff will be long gone,' said Aunt, deflated.

'Yes, but we're going to somewhere better,' said Polly. 'We've enough money to pay for a stagecoach ride there.' Polly felt the weight of the purse Mr Greg had given her, resting against her right knee. 'Mr Greg gave me enough for riding inside the coach because I said you were old.'

'What else have you told to make them want me up there?' laughed Aunt. 'Lies or truths?'

'Truths,' said Polly. 'But I maybe chose which truths to tell them. Now, where can we get you clothes that don't make it so obvious that you've come from a workhouse?'

At a pawnbroker's they found Aunt a respectable outfit that almost fitted. Polly's and Aunt's earnings together paid for that.

Soon they were squashed on to a seat facing forwards in the stagecoach that was galloping towards Manchester. As they rolled away from London and into the countryside, Aunt gazed out of the window, reminding Polly of Min's wonder on her journey north. Aunt began to hum her daddy's song to the rhythm of the swaying coach.

'A man visiting the mill knew that song,' said Polly quietly. The other passengers had their eyes closed, heads nodding.

'Well I never,' said Aunt.

'He said that a soldier sang it to him at Waterloo after the battle there.' She looked at Aunt's face to see if that caused a reaction. But Aunt was still smiling out of the window, hardly paying attention to Polly. 'Aunt,' said Polly a bit more sharply. 'You said my dad was at Waterloo.'

'Yes, that's what your mother told me.'

'Well, the man said that the soldier who sang that song was called John Freeman. Freeman like me.' Aunt's beaky face suddenly turned and looked intently at Polly. 'Is John Freeman the name of my daddy?' said Polly. 'Is he the man who was like a robin?'

'Oh, Polly,' said Aunt, her face gone white. 'I . . . I . . . Oh, goodness. I don't know anything but that your ma said he'd fought at Waterloo. So he might be.' Aunt's thin body had begun to tremble beside Polly.

'Aunt?' she said.

'I don't know, Poll. Well . . . oh . . .' Tears were

glinting down Aunt's cheeks now.

'What is it?' said Polly. 'What else do you know? Tell me!' she said, in such a fierce voice that the gentleman opposite opened his eyes.

'Is everything all right?' he asked.

They reassured him politely that all was well. Then they sat in stiff silence, each deep in their own thoughts. *Don't think that I'm not going to ask you more*, thought Polly. *What IS it that's upsetting you so?* She didn't know whether to feel sorry for trembling weepy aunt or angry with her.

For hours the coach rocked and jolted northwards. As evening darkened, they stopped at an inn for the night, and Polly and Aunt were put in a tiny bedroom on their own. Aunt sagged on to the bed, taking off her bonnet. Polly stood, looking down at her. 'Tell me!' she said, resuming where they'd left off hours earlier.

'Oh, Poll,' said Aunt setting her bonnet down. 'I should have told you everything before.' She looked pleadingly at Polly. 'But you and me, we sort of made it all up together and were happy, weren't we? And now you're getting grown-up, Poll, and of course you want more than stories. I . . . I just wonder if you'll forgive me when you know . . .'

'Know what?' said Polly, crossing her arms. 'Of course I know my ma wasn't really a swan. Only a human woman could've had a baby. Only a human could be your niece. But what about my dad?'

Aunt was twisting bony hands in her lap. 'I only met your ma, Catherine Freeman, when she came to my door one day, big-bellied and scared. She asked for help and I took her in. She gave birth to you on my bed, and she died soon after. Then it was just tiny you and me, Poll. Just the two of us. And oh, how I loved you!' Aunt looked at Polly with pleading eyes. 'I still love you better than I've ever loved any other in my life.'

'I know you love me,' said Polly, crouching down to look Aunt in the face. ''Course I do. But where was my ma from? Why was she on her own and not with my dad? And Aunt, *was* my dad John Freeman who fought at Waterloo?'

'I think he must've been,' said Aunt. 'Sit down properly, Poll, and I'll tell what I know.'

'With no adding bits or changing things,' said Polly

as she sat. 'I want the truth.'

'I promise you I'll tell it as I know it,' said Aunt. She took a deep breath, clutched her hands together, and began. 'Catherine did call out for somebody called John as she lay dying. But she told me before that her man had another name too. It were an African one that I can't remember.'

'Try!' said Polly, fierce again.

'Oh, I wish I could for you, darling! I've been thinking and thinking in the coach these past hours because I knew you'd want to know it, and I just can't.' But something else about what she'd said was striking Polly now.

'African?'

'Yes, Poll. He was from a country somewhere in Africa, see. That's what you ma told me. She said his ma was taken, along with him, when he was just a baby from that African place. Your ma said that his ma was the daughter of a chief in their land. So your grandma was a sort of a princess, and him, your dad, a prince. I didn't make that up when I said he was royalty. That was told me by Catherine. Honest.'

'But why did they get taken from their home?' said Polly.

'To be slaves, Poll,' said Aunt. 'Slaves.'

Polly closed her eyes, feeling sick. Her father. Her grandmother. Slaves.

Aunt was still talking. 'They was slaves working on a sugar plantation in Jamaica – that's ever such a hot place. The slaves' owner and boss called the baby that was your dad "John" instead of his African name. That's what your ma told me. They gave him their own surname too, but I don't know what that surname was. I don't suppose your dad wanted it remembered. Your ma said he chose "Freeman" for himself when he stopped being a slave. That was when he signed on as a soldier in the British Army. Joining the army freed him from being a slave, see, so then he could choose a name of his own. He chose Freeman for being a free man. Only he wasn't that free, because now he was in the British army and had to fight its wars.'

'Waterloo.'

'That's just the most famous battle he fought.'

'But I know he didn't die in it,' said Polly.

'No. He was hurt in it, but not killed, your ma said.

She was that proud of him, Poll. She said he was so handsome in his red jacket and all.'

'I think he sang his *olele* song to the man I met,' said Polly. She could almost feel her father taking form in her mind and heart, but of course there were so many more questions. 'When did he meet . . .'

'. . . your lovely young ma?' said Aunt, smiling as she remembered. 'She told me that John Freeman's regiment came to Scotland after that war against the French was over, and he and your ma met at a chapel service one Sunday. They fell in love and wanted to be married. He had enough money from soldiering to set her up in a place. But your ma's family wouldn't hear of them getting wed.'

'Why not?'

'Well, he was from abroad. And I'm guessing his looks and brown skin made them uncomfortable, being so different from their own. And Catherine was very young so they may have worried on that account.' Aunt chuckled. 'But you can tell that didn't stop them, can't you, Poll, because here you are! But Catherine's parents were right in a way to worry because John Freeman did get sent off soldiering again, so Catherine was on her own with the baby coming. Why they didn't stand by her when she needed them, I don't understand.' Aunt shook her head. 'They turned away their own child and the grandchild inside her. So that's when Catherine set off, on her own, all the way from Scotland to London, thinking to meet John in London when his regiment came home again. But the regiment people in London said he was abroad and they wouldn't help her. So then she was desperate, with nowhere to go. She told me she'd stood on the street, watching people pass, wondering if any of them might be kind if she asked for help. She saw me, and decided in her head that I looked kind. I don't know why, but isn't that nice?' Aunt smiled. 'Ain't nobody thought that about me before.'

'Then what?' said Polly.

'So I did help her. I took her home, and soon after that you was born, pretty as anything. And your ma lived for just few days after that, then died.' Polly realised that she was crying, thinking of her ma as a real young woman now, rather than a swan in a story.

'Did my daddy know about me?'

Aunt was silent.

'Aunt?'

'I don't want to tell you no more, Poll. Why poke around in the past, stirring things up. See, you're already crying!'

'There's something more, I know it,' said Polly. She clutched Aunt's thin arm fiercely. 'Tell me.'

'You might not like me for it,' said Aunt.

'I don't care,' said Polly. So Aunt told.

'When Catherine was with me, she asked for a pen and paper. I got, well, if I'm truth-telling, I stole them for her, because I could tell it mattered. So she wrote, all beautiful writing, to her John. She told him about you in the letter, I think. Then she had you, and died.' Aunt held Polly's gaze steadily, but her voice wobbled now. 'And I did a terrible thing after that.'

'What?'

'I betrayed her, Polly. And I betrayed you too.'

'How?'

'After Catherine died, and they'd taken her body away, I sat there with you in my arms, and I just loved you so full to bursting that I couldn't bring myself to take that letter to your daddy's regiment as I'd promised your ma I would. At first I told myself "it's too cold to take a small baby out, and there's no hurry since he's overseas anyway". But weeks passed, then months and even years . . . and I've still not done it.'

'But . . .!' Polly jumped up, glaring at Aunt, who held up her hands as if in surrender.

'By then I loved you so deep, Polly, so deep, don't you see? I couldn't bear the thought of giving you up to your daddy. So the poor man still doesn't know what happened to his Catherine or even that he had a child.'

'You stole me,' said Polly, voice steely. And Aunt didn't deny it. 'You aren't any blood relation of mine. You aren't my great-aunt at all.'

Aunt shook her head. 'I'm not. But I've always loved you so!'

'That doesn't count for anything when you lied to me about . . . about . . . ME!' said Polly, and she slammed out of the room, down the stairs and out of the inn.

Chapter 20

Hours later, Polly crept back into the dark inn bedroom, lay down on the floor, wide awake, and knew that Aunt was wide awake in the bed beside another woman who had arrived.

Polly's mind spun with thoughts. That unhappy bony old lady on the bed wasn't her real aunt. *But Min was no blood relation, yet she felt a real sister to me. Aunt cared for me better than Catherine's parents did her. What counts most, loving and caring, or being a blood relation?*

Polly realised that Aunt had never truly lied to her, only told stories she knew were stories, along with some of the truth. *But she did steal me from my daddy who might have wanted and loved me*, thought Polly, hands clenching into fists.

And now she and 'Aunt' were on their way to Quarry Bank to be together. *What am I going to do?* wondered Polly. *What AM I going to do?*

By the time sunrise lightened the sky outside the window and somebody banged on the door to tell them to get moving or the coach would go without them, Polly had made up her mind. Aunt looked warily at Polly as they all three in that bedroom gathered themselves and went downstairs. A part of Polly liked the power she had over Aunt just then. Another part of her knew that was mean of her. *But Aunt had the power to deny me my daddy for all of my life! It serves her right to make her wait now*, she thought.

She relented as they stepped outside. 'Aunt?' said Polly.

'Yes,' said Aunt, looking nervously at her.

'About you stealing me.'

'Yes?'

'Well, you always said that it doesn't count as proper stealing if you're putting something into the hands of those that'll appreciate it the most. I think you were doing that with me. Besides, you're not the only one in this world who has taken people that didn't belong to them. Those slave owners did it without the love, and that's much worse than what you did.'

'Oh, that's it!' said Aunt, taking Polly's face between her hands. 'And I'm ever so sorry about it, Poll. I was always going to post that letter, and always going to tell you, but . . .' Polly pushed Aunt's hands away.

'My dad might have loved me too,' she said. 'Get up into the coach now. Go on.'

'Do you forgive me, Pol?' whispered Aunt as the coach began to rumble along the road northwards once more. Polly didn't answer straight away.

'I might do,' she said.

The stagecoach carried them to Manchester. Then a cart took them out through countryside again to Quarry Bank Mill.

'Oh, my lor!' said Aunt as they came over the brow of a hill and heard the rumble of the great mill down below, tugging, turning, twisting, weaving cotton into cloth. Polly laughed at Aunt's reaction, but also at herself because she realised this felt more like coming home than their visit to the basement under the Proudfoots' house had been. She looked about for people she knew to wave to as the cart came to a standstill at the Apprentice House. Mrs Dawson came hurrying out, telling them to come inside for lunch, and looking at Aunt.

'Miss Brown, you're most welcome,' she said. 'You too, of course, Polly.'

That afternoon, Polly took Aunt down to Mr Greg in his office. He sent off a boy to report to Miss Flintock at Norcliffe Hall that the rose-making woman had arrived and would be ready for work next day.

Mr Greg shook Aunt's hand and offered her a seat. Aunt was keeping her mouth tight so as not to show her wonky teeth. Mr Greg sat down at his desk with papers in front of him. Polly stood beside Aunt. *All because I looked at things differently, as Aunt taught me to,* she thought with wonder.

'Now, Miss Brown,' began Mr Greg, and he went on to discuss living arrangements and pay and more. He had a big ledger open in front of him, and a paper that he was going to ask Aunt to sign. But now Polly was looking at things differently again. Mr Greg saying 'Miss Brown' to Aunt had set a new thought buzzing in her head, and it settled so firmly there that she stepped forward, interrupting the master.

'Mr Greg, sir,' she said boldly. 'While you have papers out, please can I see in writing what makes me your apprentice until I'm eighteen? I never did sign it myself so I've never seen it, and by rights I should see it, shouldn't I? Since it's about me.' Mr Greg looked startled. Polly took a step back, hands meekly behind her back now. 'Besides, my aunt would like to see it, I'm sure.' Aunt was also looking surprised, but nodded keenly when Mr Greg looked at her for assent.

'Very well,' said Mr Greg. He went to a shelf, searched, head on one side as he read things, then pulled out a scrolled and tied indenture certificate, and flattened it on to his desk for Polly and Aunt to see.

'Very nice,' said Aunt. But Polly was searching

through the curly script on the paper for a particular word. 'Brown'.

'There!' Polly jabbed a finger at the name of the apprentice. 'That says Brown, and that's not me,' she said.

'You are Polly Brown, are you not?' said Mr Greg. 'This was filled in, as I remember, by the man who brought you from the workhouse.' He looked suddenly worried at the reminder that Polly was from a workhouse. He glanced quizzically at her great-aunt.

'But I'm not Polly *Brown*,' said Polly, grinning. 'The workhouse had me down as that in their book, but I'm rightly Polly Freeman. Aunt can tell you that. So that person in writing isn't me. Which means I'm free, doesn't it?'

That took a bit of explaining.

'Are you saying that you don't want to work at Quarry Bank any more?' said Mr Greg, hand to brow as if he might have a slight headache. 'I must say that does seem somewhat ungrateful of you just when we've gone to the trouble and expense of bringing your aunt here.'

'Oh, but I do want to work here,' said Polly, hands

clasped in front of her now. 'I really do. And thank you for getting Aunt here.' She held her head up. 'But I want to be a worker what gets paid for work. And I want to know that I can leave, without having to run away and being hunted for and caught and punished. Not that I want to leave, not now, and I hope I never do again.'

'That's it,' said Aunt. 'That's what anybody'd want, isn't it?'

'It seems that you may have a fair legal point,' said Mr Greg. 'I'll look into it.'

It was arranged that Aunt and Polly would rent the back bedroom of Betsy's family's house in the village. They were to share the main room and kitchen with Betsy's family. There was a yard at the rear and an allotment growing food and flowers in front. There were curtains in the window. *Min would love this*, thought Polly.

That sunny autumn evening there was a chill in the air, but colours were vivid in the last evening light. It all felt settled and good except for one thing. There was still one big question that Polly's mind pick, pick, picked at like fingers picking oakum.

'What's on your mind?' said Aunt as they sat in their room. So Polly took a deep breath and told her.

'That letter,' said Polly. 'The one my mum wrote to my daddy. You said that you was always intending to post it.'

'I did,' said Aunt.

'Is that still true?' asked Polly. Then she almost held her breath as Aunt bent down to lift up the skirt of her dress.

'Aunt? Do you still have it?' Polly's voice was almost squeaking.

'Here,' said Aunt, taking a tired, soft, folded old piece of paper out of a pocket . . .

'. . . in your drawers!' said Polly, marvelling that Aunt had kept such a thing in her underwear all those years.

'I took the letter out whenever I washed my drawers, Poll. But drawers is the only bit of clothing of my own that they let me keep in the workhouse,' said Aunt. 'And this letter is the only thing I truly cared didn't get into the hands of that Mrs Proudfoot.'

'Let's see it,' said Polly as Aunt gently unfolded the

letter and laid it flat on the windowsill where the last of the light showed faded twirly lines of copperplate writing. 'It's beautiful,' said Polly. She tried to read it. 'That's a "J" there. For "John"?' Neither of them could read well enough to make out the rest of it. Besides, the letter was faded and worn and faint.

'We can get it read,' said Aunt. 'There's lots around here who can read, I'm sure.'

'Then can we post it? Mr Smethick knew which regiment John Freeman had moved to,' said Polly. 'D'you think he could still be a soldier? If he's even alive?'

'I just don't know, Poll. But yes, let's post it. Most likely we'll never hear anything back, but who knows?' She gave an apologetic little smile. 'I'll be glad to keep my promise to Catherine at last.'

Betsy's father read them the letter:

'My dear John, I write to you from Mell Lane in London where I am in the kind care of Miss Jemima Brown. You may wonder why I left our home. John, I am with child. That child will soon be born. I long for the three of us to be together. Come and find me on your return. And, darling John, keep safe wherever you are. Your loving wife, Catherine.'

Betsy's father wrote a letter to accompany that one from Catherine, telling more, and both letters were sealed together and sent to the headquarters of the Black Watch regiment.

Then they waited and wondered as Aunt made fine fabric flowers for the Greg ladies and their friends, and Polly embroidered or worked in the mill. She got paid a small pot of coins at the end of each week. Sometimes Aunt taught embroidery at the Apprentice House in the evenings. And, always, Aunt talked.

'Polly told us that she's royalty,' said Big Ann. 'That's not true, is it, Miss Brown?'

'Oh yes, it is,' said Aunt. 'Did she also tell you that when I was your age I was a dancer in a circus?'

'No!' said Big Ann.

'Did she tell you that I danced as naked as a newborn babe except for a fluffy pink ostrich feather or two? Did she say that I did my dancing on top of an elephant, and that I played the maracas and sang, all while balancing a big ball on me head?' said Aunt.

'No, she never did!' said Big Ann, mouth agape.

'Well, that's because none of that ever happened!' cackled Aunt, her wonky teeth on full display. Polly, Little Ann and the others all laughed at that, and so did Mrs Dawson.

At home, in their room, Polly and Aunt sewed something else. They saved scraps of fabric, working them together into a patchwork cover for their bed. It wasn't a patchwork of regular shapes. This was a bright jumble of colours and shapes that they worked in a piece at a time.

'Because life doesn't always come together neat and orderly and how we might think that we want it,' said Aunt.

'But it can still be pretty,' said Polly.

Historical
Afterword

When I read a story set in the past, I like to know which bits of this story are based on truth, and which parts are total fiction. This is where I explain those truths and untruths.

St Pancras Workhouse was a real place experienced by many thousands of poor people. Robert Blincoe wrote a memoir account of his own childhood time in St Pancras Workhouse some years before my fictional Polly is sent there. The building had changed since his time, but much about life there remained the same. That workhouse housed about five hundred inmates, many of them working at oakum picking, stone breaking, or doing laundry work, and sleeping in large dormitories, three to a bed. A plan of the workhouse shows large 'Imbecile and Lunatic Wards' for those with mental health problems.

At the age of seven, the real boy Robert, was sent from St Pancras Workhouse to work as a scavenger at a cotton mill in Nottingham. He tells that the children were promised roast beef and plum pudding, silver pocket watches and rides in the master's carriage. That was all lies. Instead, they had to work fourteen hours a day six days a week in dangerous, hard conditions, eating only small portions of porridge. Robert ran away from that mill but was brought back. He went on to work at another cotton mill, surviving to finish his apprenticeship, but with half a finger torn off in an accident with mill machinery. Robert then set up his own spinning business. He wrote his memoir to help publicise the plight of poor children working in the mills. That campaign helped lead to the 1833 Factory Act that prevented children under nine years old being employed in factories any more. Charles Dickens is said

to have based his *Oliver Twist* character partly on Robert Blincoe's experiences.

Quarry Bank Mill is real, and you can visit the Apprentice House, and mill, and the village of Styal, where you can see and feel where Polly lived and worked.

Samuel Greg came to England from Ireland, and he had Quarry Bank Mill built at the end of the eighteenth century. At the time of this story, Quarry Bank Mill was run by his son, Robert Hyde Greg. Robert had a wife and six children, including Hannah, known as Sophy, who appears in this story.

Quarry Bank Mill used a lot of child workers. Why? Because children were cheap to employ, and they were small enough to do those scavenging and piecing jobs under the machinery that adults were too big to do. But there was also a shortage of adult labour. Most adults worked in farming jobs, growing

food. War with France meant that many able-bodied men were away, fighting. But the Industrial Revolution was creating thousands of new jobs. Some years before this story, prime minister William Pitt had suggested that the country needed to 'yoke up the children' to do that factory work. Workhouses had lots of orphans and abandoned children in them. Factories needed the strongest of those children as workers. The parish authorities who ran the workhouses wanted to have fewer people to care and pay for. So parishes actually paid factories to take children from workhouses. They paid Robert Hyde Greg two guineas for every child that he took off them in the 1840s. Most of Quarry Bank's apprentice children came from workhouses in Liverpool, so Polly is a bit of an odd one out, coming from London. Children were also sent from workhouses to work in British colonies abroad, in Canada,

South Africa and Australia. They were offered as free labour to farmers and others settling in those places. Orphan children from Britain were sent to work in Australia as recently as 1967, so in my lifetime.

The purpose of Quarry Bank Mill was to process raw cotton into thread, and then weave that into cloth. Cotton plants were grown, and the cotton harvested from them, in America. In 1838, the hard fieldwork was still largely done by slaves who had been taken from African countries. The cotton was packed into large bales, then shipped across the Atlantic Ocean to the port of Liverpool on the west coast of England. From there the bales were taken by canal barge or wagon inland to Quarry Bank Mill.

In the mill, the cotton was pulled from the bales, then put through scutching and carding machines to pick out seeds and sticks. The

machines then pulled and twisted the cotton into 'rovings' of soft clean cotton ready for spinning.

Polly mostly works on one of the spinning floors of the mill. Each of those spinning floors were lined with many spinning mules. A mule would 'draw' its carriage, pulling over a thousand lines of threads, back and forth to stretch and twist the cotton into threads. Children had to move fast to get under the mules, clear flue off the machinery, and then get back out from under before the carriage returned. When threads broke, a piecer had to twist the broken ends of the thread together again. It is reckoned that a piecer would walk about twenty miles a day as they went from mule to mule.

On another floor of the mill there were sixty weaving looms powered by a new steam engine. What was made at Quarry Bank

was a fairly rough calico cotton fabric, not fine enough for clothing for the Greg family. Their cotton clothing would have been made of linen or muslin, or they would have worn woollen or silk fabrics.

Samuel Greg had chosen to build Quarry Bank Mill on the River Bollin so that he could make use of the waterpower. Controlled by a weir and head-race and sluice gates, the river's flowing water powered the mill's machinery by turning great waterwheels. By 1838 there were two waterwheels, and the newest of those was the biggest waterwheel in the whole of Europe, giving power equivalent to a hundred horses. A complex system of cogs, wheels, pulleys, shafts and leather drive bands connected the thousands of spindles to that power.

Cotton is easier to work in hot, damp conditions, so the mill was deliberately made hot, keeping windows closed in the summer

and heating with paraffin heaters when weather got cold. Steam was let into the air, adding to the cotton flue to make it even more dangerous to breathe in. Because the mill was so noisy with the sound of twenty thousand wheels and spindles, nobody would hear you if you spoke, so workers created a language of hand signals and making faces, and they became fluent at lip-reading.

Some children lived with their families in the workers' cottages in the village, but many of the apprentice children lived in the Apprentice House run by a superintendent.

In 1838 there were more than ninety apprentice children living in the Apprentice House. More than sixty girls slept in shared box beds in one big room. About thirty boys slept in smaller rooms. Quarry Bank took on more girls than boys because girls were seen as being more biddable than boys, and they

were cheaper workers to pay for than men were once they became adult. Polly lives in the Apprentice House at its fullest. A few years later almost all the apprentices had gone. Robert Hyde Greg decided that apprentices cost too much to house and care for, and he would rather employ children from families in Styal village, where parents took care of the children.

As well as bedrooms upstairs, the Apprentice House has a big schoolroom downstairs, and that is probably where the children ate as well as where they were taught. If you visit that room you can see the wooden weights that children had to hold, with arms outstretched, as punishment. The Greg family didn't believe in beating children. That was unusual at the time.

There is a comfortable Superintendent's parlour, where I've imagined that Dr Holland

might have seen his apprentice child patients.

There is a big kitchen, with two big boiler pots in the corners where large quantities of porridge or scouse would have been boiled up. The food the children got here was much better than children were fed at other mills. Robert Blincoe described much worse at the mills where he worked, with children desperately scrabbling to eat turnip peelings that had been put into the pig trough. The Gregs had a farm that provided milk and butter and cheese, as well as fresh vegetables and some meat. Breakfast of porridge was eaten down at the mill, probably served in a dollop straight into whichever hand wasn't your 'cack hand'. 'Cack' means poo, and you kept one hand for wiping your bottom and the other for handling food.

Outside the Apprentice House is a yard with a pump, and there are privies (outside toilets)

and a wash house. There is also a garden where vegetables and herbs were grown.

Apprentice children had to walk two miles to church in Wilmslow and back, sometimes twice, every Sunday. But workers who lived in the village, and the Greg family themselves, went to one of the two chapels in Styal village. That was because the law said that apprentice children should go to a Church of England church because the Church of England form of Christianity was the state religion. The chapels were non-conformist, one of them Methodist and one Unitarian.

Quarry Bank was a better place to be an apprentice than many other mills, but some children still wanted their freedom. Over the years, over a hundred apprentice children ran away. Notices would be put into newspapers, describing the runaway child and offering a reward for their return. The standard reward

for returning an apprentice in the 1820s was five shillings. A written account shows one runaway girl being punished by being shut into the attic of the Apprentice House, as Polly is. But that real girl had to share the attic with the body of a dead woman!

Adult mill workers and their children lived in Styal village, a short walk from the mill, and up in cleaner air. The Gregs had most of the village houses built in the 1820s. They were terraced cottages of 'two up, two down', meaning two rooms upstairs, and two downstairs rooms. But they also had large cellar rooms underneath, reached by steps down from the road. Those cellars, with their own stoves and sinks and cupboards built in, were often lived in by another family. The houses had back yards with water butts and privies, and gardens and allotments to the front where people could grow their own vegetables

and flowers. You can still see original cooking ranges with flower decoration cast on to their iron doors. There was wallpaper on the walls. The village had its own school, and a bakery and shop, as well as the two chapels.

The cost of renting one of those cottages in 1834 was two shillings and ninepence a week. Some families sub-let one of the bedrooms, as Betsy's family do for Polly and Aunt in my story. To rent the cellar cost one shilling a week. As a percentage of the money the workers earned, the cost of renting those houses was less than it is for many people working and renting today. A spinner was paid fourteen shillings for a seventy-hour working week at that time. That was the best-paid job below manager level. If Polly had been paid a wage rather than being an apprentice child, she would have been paid one shilling and sixpence a week.

Dr Peter Holland was a real doctor. He

was the Greg family's doctor who was then employed by them to take medical care of their workers. The Gregs looked after their workers better than most mill employers did. Of course, that helped to keep those workers working productively, as well as being the kind thing to do. Dr Holland was a man of over seventy at the time of this story. He checked all children arriving to become apprentices to ensure that they were healthy. Min would normally have been turned away because she was already suffering from tuberculosis, also known as 'consumption' or 'mill fever'. But once she was working at the mill, she would have been just one of many who coughed a lot because breathing in the cotton fibres destroyed everybody's lungs.

Dr Holland's test to see whether a child was over the age of nine and therefore legally allowed to work in a mill was to get them

to reach an arm over the top of their head and touch the ear lobe on the other side. He thought that children under the age of nine couldn't reach their ear there. Each child was vaccinated against smallpox. Dr Holland kept careful records of the names of those treated, and with what medicines. For example, many children got sore eyes from the cotton flue in the air in the mill. The redness of their sore eyes was blood in inflamed arteries, so it was thought that those children had too much blood in their bodies. The cure used for that was to attach leeches to the child's neck to suck out some blood. Leeches have three mouths each and over a hundred tiny teeth that latch on and suck blood. Of course, that didn't actually help the sore eyes at all. But washing the eyes in an eyewash made from camomile flowers might well have helped to sooth them. Many children got injured, hit by

flying shuttles, or fingers caught in machinery. Many suffered from having lungs clogged with cotton flue that left them short of oxygen, and grey-faced. But at least they were given some care.

Polly's father, John Freeman, is made-up but I based him on Sergeant George Rose who was real. George Rose's army discharge papers show that he joined the 73rd Foot Regiment of the British army in 1809. That regiment was in Jamaica because Jamaica was part of the British Empire at that time. But British-born soldiers got ill, and some died there, so it was quite usual for the army to recruit strong young men from the island. Young men who were slaves were often keen to join the British army because becoming a soldier gave them freedom from slavery, even if they were then owned by the army for however many years the army wanted them. Slaves were often given their owner's surname, but they could choose to change their name once they were free. 'Freeman' was a name that many chose, identifying their new status. That's why I chose that surname for Polly's father.

The real George Rose was twenty-four when he fought at the Battle of Waterloo in 1815. He was badly injured during the fighting. In the years that followed, he married a British wife and had children, and he served in various places around the world. He was discharged from the army in 1837. In 1849 he returned to Jamaica as a Methodist missionary. Slavery had been abolished in most of the British Empire by then. George Rose died near where he had been born.

Before my story begins, Samuel Greg and his brother had inherited a half share each in owning seventy-one male and sixty-eight female enslaved people. Those enslaved

people lived and worked on a sugar plantation in the Caribbean. When slavery was abolished in that part of the British Empire, the British government paid large sums of money to British slave owners such as the Gregs for the loss of their 'property'. But the enslaved people themselves didn't get paid anything at all.

Slavery continued in America where the Quarry Bank cotton came from until 1865.

There are still people held in slavery in the world today, working without either proper pay or freedom. Some of those enslaved people are children.

Polly's 'daddy's song' is in a language called Lingala, and is sung as a lullaby or by canoe paddlers singing to their paddle strokes. It comes from the Congo in the middle of Africa. I'm imagining that it had travelled with Polly's African grandmother from the

west coast of Africa to the Caribbean. I don't actually know whether or not it is an old enough song to have been around at that time.

So, as you can see, this story is a twisting together of threads of true history and threads of imagination.

Pippa Goodhart

FINDING FORTUNE

"Please do not be cross. The fact is, I am to go with Fa to Canada. It is my idea, and not his. Mama always said that one should live every moment of life. That is what I am doing."

Ida's mother has died, leaving her in the charge of her beloved Fa - only it seems like Ida's the one who does most of the caring. When Fa decides to travel to the Klondike in search of gold, leaving Ida in the care of her Grandmama, Ida knows she mustfind a way to go with him.

The sights and sounds of the journey and the hardships they face will push them to very limit of human endurance - and change them forever.

FINDING FORTUNE
Pippa Goodhart
$800 CLAIM
$8000 CLAIM
ALASKA
$20,000 CLAIM
$100,000
$1,000,000
FIELDS
DAWSON
SIXTY MILE
$75,000
$10,000 CLAIM
McMillan River
Pelly River
CHILKOOT PASS
SKAGWAY
YUKUTAT

RAVEN BOY

Legend has it that if the ravens leave the Tower of London, then monarch and kingdom will fall.

London 1666: the Great Plague rages and the city is a dangerous place. Young Nick Truelove blames his King, Charles II, for the hardships he faces and vows to get revenge. Inspired by the bold behaviour and wily cunning of a young raven, Nick bluffs his way into the centre of the King's power - the Tower of London itself. But, as a remarkable friendship grows between boy and raven, a new danger engulfs London. Nick's view of the world and his King is about to be changed forever.

THE GREAT SEA DRAGON DISCOVERY

Cambridge, 1860

Bill's head is full of questions and it always seems to get him into trouble. Especially when one of his experiments causes his father to lose his job. Bill gets a bit of money for his family selling interesting fossils he has found, but then someone else needs his help and fast. It just so happens that Bill has discovered something that could be the answer to his problems. But for the rest of the world, it is something that questions everything...